"You can't...

haven't even tasted your tea."

He looked down his nose, refusing to be charmed. "My purpose in coming here is duty, not pleasure," he said, being his most priggish. "Lady Sarah has bid me inform you that I am to escort you both to tonight's entertainment at Haversham Hall. She seems to feel I shall be a steadying influence, there to fend off any trouble you might otherwise find."

"I see," she said stiffly, but he thought he saw a flash of rebellion in those remarkably green eyes.

Geoff paused at the door to deliver a parting shot. "Oh, and do try to be ready by nine. There's nothing more loathsome, I find, than a female who keeps a man waiting."

He was quite certain she huffed as he sailed out of the room. Splendid. By the time he arrived tonight—not until well past ten—he'd have her seething. One skillfully placed taunt, and she'd do most anything to defy him . . .

Love and Honor

Barbara Benedict

J

JOVE BOOKS, NEW YORK

LOVE AND HONOR

A Jove Book / published by arrangement with
the author

PRINTING HISTORY
Jove edition / February 1994

ISBN: 0-515-11312-3

A JOVE BOOK®
Jove Books are published by The Berkley Publishing Group,
200 Madison Avenue, New York, New York 10016.
JOVE and the "J" design are trademarks belonging to Jove Publications, Inc.

PRINTED IN THE UNITED STATES OF AMERICA

10 9 8 7 6 5 4 3 2 1

Prologue

"Dull, dull, dull."

Lady Sarah, the dowager countess of Fairbright, scanned the list of upcoming engagements with blatant disdain. Once, she'd lifted up her invitations with delicious anticipation, yet of late, each envelope she opened brought on a migraine. After one more mind-dulling night at Almack's—or worse, at some musicale where simpering females warbled like tropical birds—and Sarah would retire from the Season for good.

Unfortunately, however, she had nowhere to go. With her nephew Richard soon marrying, she could no longer repair to Fairbright Manor, the family's country estate. Sarah might be selfish and set in her ways, but even she knew that Richard and his Andrea Gratham wanted—and deserved—a good year to themselves.

She smiled, remembering the devious manner in which she had brought the pair together. Matchmaking was such fun—and she was quite good at it, too. Perhaps she could . . .

Suddenly excited, she considered this intriguing pastime. In all of London, there must be someone who could benefit from her expertise, some poor soul who had yet to find the perfect mate. But who?

Leaning on her cane, she rose to her feet, ignoring the creak of aging bones. Her nephew Horatio had yet to wed, but the thought of saddling any female with that jackanapes quite turned her stomach.

Honor Drummond. As the name popped into her head, Sarah smiled like a cat with its mouse. Too well, she could remember the ruckus her great-niece and goddaughter had kicked up during her last stint upon the town. Indeed, Honor had been so scandalous, her father had been compelled to banish her to an aunt in Scotland.

Crossing to the bellpull, Sarah rang for her butler, determined to summon General Drummond at once. Honor's exile had gone on long enough, she would inform the man; it was time they found his girl a husband.

And all that remained was to choose who the lucky man would be.

$$\approx 1 \approx$$

Intent upon stealing a nap—a difficult proposition here in Pithnevel House—Geoff pounded the cushions of his aunt Maude's immense sofa into a more amenable position. He'd chosen the library for refuge, as it was far away from his uncle's study, and this sofa, since it faced the shelves and not the door. If found by his uncle Cyrus, Geoff knew he'd be forced to listen at length about how sorely he'd been neglecting his new responsibilities.

Becoming an earl, in Geoff's opinion, was not quite what he'd been led to expect. What use was the extra income if he must sink his cash into the hopelessly run-down Lennox Hall? Was he to blame that the previous earl, in drowning his sorrows at the death of his young wife, had let the estate—and himself—go to ruin?

I've my own sorrows to drown, Geoff thought irritably as he stretched out on the sofa. What of all the years he'd spent learning to be a ne'er-do-well, in perfecting the life of a Dissolute? Merely because some distant relative choked on a chicken bone, must his pleasantly selfish existence vanish forever?

Uncle Cyrus certainly seemed to think so. As did Aunt

Maude, with her endless parade of eligible females, all touting marriage as if it were some magic elixir to settle him down.

Hands cradling his head, Geoff scowled at the ceiling. Thank heavens they could not know how close he had come to actually making an offer. How humiliating, to have the woman of his heart turn to his best friend, Richard, instead.

As he thought of Andrea Gratham, Geoff's heart gave a twist. He'd always imagined Andy would be there waiting, when and if he chose to wed, but alas, the invitation on the hallway table proved how foolish he had been. They'd make a handsome couple, Richard and Andy. Geoff couldn't deny it, but drat it all, must he always find himself the odd man out?

Life is too short to waste on self-pity, he told himself as he punched the pillows again; he might as well sleep. A tiresome business, this heartache.

"Who?" his cousin Iris said outside the door. "Tell me, Hermione. Who is coming to town?"

Her sister sighed. "Oh, it's too delicious to share. I think I shall make you wait for Papa's announcement."

Wishing himself invisible, Geoff wondered how he could have thought the library a refuge. No place was safe as long as those gossipmongers roamed the halls.

His cousins still retained hopes that they might yet snare a husband, but in the three Seasons Iris and Hermione had been thrust upon the poor ton, neither had come within an arm's length of an offer. Although they'd certainly tried their worst on his good friends, Foxley and Bellington.

"You'd best tell me at once," Iris demanded, stomping a foot, "or I shall tell Papa you were eavesdropping outside his study door again."

"Tattle-box," Hermione hissed through the spaces between her teeth. "Very well, but not here by the door. I don't wish the servants to overhear."

Groaning inwardly, Geoff sank deeper into the generous cushions, hoping he might yet escape discovery. His cousins were nothing if not vocal, and considering the brandy he'd consumed the night before, he'd as soon forego their shrieks of alarm.

Geoff braced himself as a log dropped in the fire, making noise enough to wake the dead, but the girls settled without a whimper into the winged chairs before the hearth. Intent upon their gossip, they'd no doubt fail to hear a cannon exploding at their ears.

"If you must know, Iris, Papa has been speaking with Lord Frampton."

"Frampton, of the War Office? Oh my, then that horrid Napoleon truly did escape? You cannot mean it is he who is coming to town?"

Hermione snorted. "Pea goose, as if anyone cares about the political mayhem men love to create. It's the social scene I speak of, sister dear. This Season promises to be the most titillating ever."

Geoff, whose interest had been piqued by the mention of the Corsican, settled back down in disgust.

"Do get on with your tale, Hermione, or I swear I shall scream down the house."

Again Geoff braced himself, but Hermione forestalled any scream by dangling the proverbial carrot before her sibling's equine face. "You shall do nothing of the sort if you hope to hear the whole of it. At last, Frampton has offered us a means for revenge. Or don't you wish to see our cousin suffer for telling Lord Foxley you snore?"

"Of course I want revenge. But never say Frampton means to send Geoffrey to fight the French?"

With a surge of euphoria, Geoff thought of tearing across some battlefield, brandishing a sword. Like most men, he liked to imagine himself as the dashing knight, rushing in to save the day, or rescuing his damsel in distress.

Hermione dampened such woolgathering with a snort of contempt. "As the earl, Geoffrey can hardly be risked to the vagaries of war. Heavens, Iris, don't you listen? He and Papa argue over this constantly."

Iris sighed—though not as heavily as Geoff—and voiced the question that was currently on his mind. "Then pray tell, just what *are* you talking about?"

"Honor Drummond."

And for Geoff, it was as if a cannon had indeed exploded in their midst. He sat up, oblivious to the girls' presence, or even the pounding in his brandy-bruised skull. A cold rage swept over him as though it were now, and not five years earlier, that the female had made him feel an absolute fool.

Returning from abroad that Season, Geoff had just come into town to celebrate the imminent wedding of his good friend, Jeremy Wharton. Perhaps he'd already celebrated too much, for when this adorable female came racing out of Lady Sarah's town house, spinning some yarn about a mortally ill relative while tearfully pleading for a ride to the nearest coach station, he'd suddenly seen himself as her knight in armor and had proved only too happy to comply.

It wasn't until he'd begun to drive off, and General Drummond hailed them from behind, that Geoff recalled such things as propriety and logic—and a father's righteous wrath. As he stood there trying to defend himself from the general, and an equally distressed Jeremy Wharton—from whom, it turned out, Miss Drummond was running—the heartless miss slipped quietly away. There had been no thanks, nor regret; she'd skipped off and let Geoff shoulder the blame.

"Honor Drummond cannot be returning to London," Iris was saying, echoing Geoff's thoughts a second time. "She's been banished to Scotland."

"*Had* been. When one thinks of the misery she caused her poor father with her scandalous behavior, the general must be a saint to reconsider. Were I her parent, I can tell you, she could spend the rest of her days with those Highland barbarians, as that is plainly where she belongs."

If Iris was like a horse, Hermione could be a great busy hen, ever ready to preen over others' misfortunes. Though in Miss Drummond's case, Geoff quickly amended, the clucking was clearly justified.

"But I don't understand, Hermione. What has any of this to do with Geoff?"

He leaned closer, likewise curious.

"Well," Hermione's tone went conspiratorial, though not one whit lowered in volume, "Frampton served with the general on the Continent and now wishes to help. Unfortunately, with no suitable female relations, Frampton is unable to provide his friend's daughter with the necessary companionship."

"I cannot see how Geoffrey—"

"Not Geoffrey, you ninnyhammer. Miss Drummond will go about with us. You and I, Iris, are to lend her an air of respectability."

"No!"

Disconcerting, how he and Iris again shared the same thought but it was downright unnerving to find he'd voiced the denial aloud.

And this time, both cousins screeched. Wincing at the noise, Geoff rose from the sofa. No help for it; he might as well involve himself in their conversation now.

"You have stooped to a new low, Geoffrey Stone." Stiff with indignation, Hermione also rose to her feet, her nose so high in the air, it seemed likely to bleed. "Eavesdropping on our coze. Shame on you!"

"Not a bit of it," he said airily, stretching his face in an unconvincing yawn. "I was taking a nap. You woke me with all your cackling."

There was nothing he enjoyed better than ruffling their feathers, which was why, perhaps, he'd told Foxley and Bellington about the snores.

Hermione, invariably the spokeswoman, took it upon herself to put him in his place. "Be that as it may, none of this is of any concern to you. As soon as the repairs are done on Lennox Hall, you will be taking yourself away."

"Oh, I don't know, I might delay. I find the prospect of entertaining Miss Drummond to be quite intriguing." He thought nothing of the kind, of course, but who could resist the jibe?

"Over my corpse. I will have you know, Iris and I have decided to take her under our wings. We mean to see that you and your rakehell ways shan't get within a pinky's length of the poor girl."

The look of horror on Iris's face proved that this was the first she'd heard of said decision. "But Honor Drummond, Hermione?" she wheezed. "Have you forgotten the talk?"

"According to Frampton, Iris, the girl is quite reformed. Her aunt Regina is a staunch Calvinist, don't you know, and it is said she now has Miss Drummond so meek and humble, the girl's own father barely recognized her."

"But, Hermione, she ran rings around the duennas the general hired. She gambled, making wagers on nearly everything. Why, there was even talk of a duel!"

Flashing her pale eyes in Geoff's direction, Hermione spoke in her sweetest tone. "Never fear, under our influence, Miss Drummond will become such a model of propriety, I daresay we shall soon be the talk of the town."

Geoff snorted. If his cousins became the talk of London, it would only be because Honor Drummond ran rings about them, too. "A leopard does not lose its spots overnight, Herm," he felt moved to advise. "You might be wiser to cut yourselves loose while you can."

"And leave her to your untender mercies? I should think not. Iris and I mean to have her wed by June."

Since Aunt Maude was a right enough sort, and Uncle Cyrus—though a bit high in the instep—at least knew reality when it glared in his face, it went beyond Geoff's comprehension how their daughters could be such dolts. "You're taking a great deal too much upon yourself, Herm. The girl is nothing but trouble. Why, I daresay I could prove in no time at all that she's no more reformed than I."

He'd meant only to offer advice, but Hermione took it as an affront. "You're always so eager to offer an opinion," she snapped. "One wonders if you're as willing to stand behind your boasts."

"You cannot mean a wager? My, my, Herm. I thought you were of the opinion that decent people never gamble."

Hermione puffed up again, a clear sign she was rattled, yet determined not to show it. No doubt she now remembered how often she'd lost at similar challenges. "It can hardly be considered gambling when family members are involved. It is rather more a . . . a friendly exchange."

"I see." Geoff quelled a grin, intrigued by how far she might take this. "And just how friendly do you intend to make it?"

"I beg your pardon?"

"The wager, Herm. How much is it to be?"

"You are too provoking, Geoffrey. We have no wish to take your coins. I suggest we trade favors instead."

"Indeed?"

"Indeed. On your part, you must contrive some way to

convince Lords Bellington and Foxley to stand up with us. We do adore dancing."

As Hermione turned to smile triumphantly at her sister, Geoff shook his head. It would be hard to induce Jamie and Adam to stay in the same room with them. Besides, the pair would be all but glued to the Gratham twins, who waited for their sister's wedding to Richard before announcing their own matrimonial plans. Still, if his cousins had no idea of the imminent death of their hopes, Geoff was not the one to tell them. He knew the fate of he who bore ill tidings.

Too, he was relieved they hadn't asked for his horses, as would have been the request of any male acquaintance. They were like family to him, his grays, and he could not like to think of his team in his cousins' hands. "Agreed," he said quickly, not willing to risk that they might yet reconsider. "And what shall I receive if Miss Drummond should *not* wed?"

"Oh, she shall."

Their gloating expressions killed any doubts he'd had about the wisdom of such a wager. He'd have taken most anything in payment, for the sheer joy of proving them wrong.

Still, he saw no sense in wasting an opportunity. "Time will tell. However, should you lose, I want the Pithnevel Pearls."

"Never!"

From the day their grandmother had left the necklace to his cousins, Geoff had tried to gain ownership. It was not that he coveted the worthless strand of mismatched globes; it had merely become a game to wrestle them from Hermione's grasp. "It is just as I thought," he said to provoke them. "You've less faith in your claim than I."

Hermione stiffened, then flashed a tight, unconvincing smile. "Very well, wretch. The Pithnevel Pearls it is."

As they shook hands, a prickling along his skin drew Geoff's gaze to the door. His uncle Cyrus stood there, silently watching.

Pithnevel's expression revealed nothing, but from past experience, Geoff knew a great deal could be concealed within that deceptively thin frame. Many was the lecture Geoff had received on the pitfalls of gambling—only this time, he had involved the man's daughters.

"If you would come to my study," his uncle told him in a voice twice as daunting for its softness. "There is a matter you and I need to discuss."

Upon which he turned and marched with quiet precision down the hall.

❧ 2 ❧

"The town house to our right belongs to the Pithnevels," Frampton was saying in his nasal tones. "I do hope you will find time to call on them later in the week. Hermione and Iris will provide excellent companionship for you."

On her side of the barouche, Honor Drummond smiled weakly. It was kind of Lord Frampton to take the time to show her about town, but deep in her heart, she couldn't help wishing her father had chosen to see to the task instead.

She tried to make excuses. General Drummond was busy at the War Office—what with this talk of Napoleon—and his numerous business ventures took up so much of his time.

Yet in her heart, she knew these same justifications could be applied to Frampton. The sad truth was that her father preferred to avoid her. Out of sight, out of mind—that was how the general always dealt with his only child.

Growing up in the country with no company but an odd assortment of tutors, Honor had assumed that all fathers so scrupulously maintained separate residences. This was not to say she had never longed that the general would tarry on his annual inspection, that he would just once glance twice at the sweater she'd tried to knit, or the watercolor she'd struggled to compose; it was merely that she'd had nothing with which to compare her existence, and as such, she'd accepted what crumbs of affection the general tossed her way.

It was not until her come-out in London that she'd seen how some parents doted on their children, that other families shared their lives and dreams on a daily basis. It was easy to see now how the gambling and racing—all her exploits really—had been but a misguided attempt to gain her father's attention. She'd wanted him to notice her, to love her. In truth, it was all she had ever wanted.

She must have sighed, for Frampton looked up with concern. "Tired, my dear? I suppose we should get you home. Can't have you falling asleep tonight at the ballet. The baron would never trust you in my care again."

Squeezing her hands in her lap, Honor forced another feeble smile. It took all her will not to cry out, "Hang the baron!" Poor Frampton would be shocked, for like everyone else, he believed Honor wanted her approaching marriage.

And she had, back in Scotland. Faced with the choice of another five years under Aunt Regina's puritan control, or the general's choice of a husband, any marriage would seem a godsend. Too, she'd hoped it would lead her father to look upon her with favor, but Baron August von Studhoff proved to be an overbearing prig, while the general, with matters settled to his satisfaction, paid her less heed than ever.

"Perhaps we should be getting home," she told Frampton meekly enough, for she'd promised the general that this time in London, she would be the model daughter—a prodigal bride, as it were—and whatever might happen, she would not be distracted from playing the role to perfection.

As Frampton ordered the coachman to turn back for Drummond House, Honor told herself that being obedient and pliable should not be all that difficult a proposition. Why, most women did it all the time. And if those wives were not precisely happy, at least they were not as lonely as she.

I should have married Jeremy, she thought, feeling a twinge of regret, and then guilt, as she thought of how her rejected suitor had died in the war.

"Oh, look," Frampton said next to her. "There goes . . ."

He was chattering on about some other notable she truly ought to know better, but Honor barely heard, lost in thought of poor Jeremy Wharton. How young and ill-prepared she'd been to cope with the gangly youth her father had selected. How could she tell the tongue-tied stranger that she longed for love, that she couldn't face life with nothing whatever to say to each other? It would be far simpler, she'd decided with adolescent logic, to just run away.

Hers had been a panicked flight that night, and all she had seen in that slightly inebriated gentleman was the means for escape. It wasn't until later, in the long five years of exile, that she had time to rue that she'd never looked at her rescuer's face.

"There are three things from which a gentleman can never run," he'd told her when she begged him to take her away, "a damsel in distress, a sure bet, and whatever coil the first two land him in."

"What was that, my dear?"

Honor started, realizing she must have mumbled aloud. "Uh, nothing," she told Frampton quickly, biting her lip. Reiterating those words had become a bad habit. What did she hope? That if she used them often enough, like some incantation, her gallant rescuer would then reappear?

Looking around her, she shook her head. It was absurd to think she would ever see him again. London was too large a town, and so much could happen in five years' time. And even if she should bump into the man, how would she know him?

All she had were his words, stating the three things from which he would never flee.

Geoff was repeating those three things in his head as he followed into Pithnevel's study. Uncle Jack, the rogue from which Geoff had learned all his tricks, had given him those guidelines years ago. If Jack had not already died from a bad liver, he'd be the first to applaud Geoff's bet with his cousins. Such a sure thing was worth any ruckus their father might now kick up. Honor Drummond, married? The Pithnevel Pearls were all but his.

But as Pithnevel went to his desk, gesturing to what his nephew had long ago terms the "interrogation" chair, Geoff nonetheless felt a trifle uneasy. Slowly, he grew aware of how the pristine state of the room contrasted with his own rather unkempt condition. The first thing any gapeseed learned upon coming to London was that appearance was all. Yet here Geoff was with creases in his trousers, and far too many wrinkles in his shirt.

Instantly on the defensive, he asked himself just how he was expected to look when he'd garnered fewer than three hours sleep? Rudely awakened by the maids banging about in the next room, he'd been in no frame of mind to don fresh linen, much less shave. He'd wanted only a nap and everyone in this dratted household seemed intent upon preventing it.

All defiance wilted as he faced Pithnevel and felt that sense of inadequacy his uncle alone could inspire.

Pithnevel had no need to go on at length about his nephew's failings; he need only stand there and set an example. Confound it, but how could any one man continue to be so impossibly noble in so unassuming a fashion?

And nowhere was this aspect of his uncle's personality more apparent than here in his study. Where others would display their achievements for the world to see, Pithnevel left his walls and desktop bare. Though as rich as a nabob, able to equip himself with every luxury, his furniture was of ungarnished oak, the wall panels a simple pine, and the draperies a wool more functional than flamboyant.

His uncle might appear as Spartan as his furnishings, but Geoff had come to realize there was a wealth of undertones to both man and room. Careful snooping revealed a volume of Shakespeare's more romantic poetry sitting on the shelves between the treatises on war, while a miniature of a smiling Aunt Maude lay tucked amid the myriad awards and commendations in a bottom drawer.

Looking up, Geoff found him posed behind his desk, arms clasped behind his back like a general regarding his troops.

"It is time you found direction," Pithnevel began. Here it comes, Geoff thought.

He should have known by now that his uncle would take the unexpected track. "I warned you years ago to offer for Miss Gratham, or risk losing her to another."

Geoff stiffened. "We both know I was too young for marriage then. Too involved with life about town."

"The fact remains," Pithnevel said, his gaze unwavering, "the decision was made. Moping now is a waste of time."

"I never mope!" Geoff straightened in the chair. For his uncle to assume that he was anything less than at the top of his mettle rankled no end.

Yet as was always the case, the more he found himself

lacking in his uncle's eyes, the more determined Geoff became to prove the man right. "If it's marriage you want," he snapped, "I daresay I could find a willing opera dancer."

Pithnevel calmly dismissed this for the absurdity it was. "Who you marry is a matter for your own conscience. I am more concerned with how you fill your time, not your household. I mean to offer you a position."

"A position?" Geoff was instantly suspicious. "Where? Doing what?"

"With me. Working for the War Office."

Stunned speechless, Geoff watched his uncle flash a rare smile. It did nothing to reassure him.

"The position requires a certain tact and discretion," Pithnevel continued. "And perhaps charm. The last of which I'm told you possess in abundance."

Geoff's imagination bloomed. A position in Vienna, perhaps? A liaison between the negotiators, each country's agents turning to him for advice? He beamed with surprised delight.

"We need someone to keep watch over a certain female," his uncle went on. "To make certain she comes to no harm."

"Female?" Geoff blinked. "What female?"

"I believe you have met her. General Drummond's daughter, Honoria."

Geoff should have known this was coming, but distracted by thoughts of Vienna, he'd overlooked just who was coming to town. "No," he said at once. "I rather think not."

"You are too much given to snap decisions, boy. At least do me the courtesy of thinking this through."

Not liking how his uncle peered down at him, Geoff stood, reversing the situation. "I have no need to think it over. It won't do. It won't do at all."

"Why?"

Why indeed? "I have no desire to play nanny to some rich brat. Honor Drummond, for lud's sakes. The girl has a remarkable talent for trouble, and we both know I can find enough on my own." So said, he turned to go.

"If you're concerned about that business five years ago, I can assure you the girl is quite reformed. She is now quite above hailing a stranger's carriage."

Geoff wheeled back to face his uncle. "You know of that incident?"

"I have worked with Drummond for years. It is only natural he would tell me."

"Indeed." Inwardly, Geoff squirmed, knowing he must have sunk to a new low in his uncle's eyes. "Can you then tell me how the man accepts me for his daughter's watchdog? Isn't it rather like hiring the fox to guard the henhouse?"

"Actually, he won't be advised of your part in this. You shall be dealing instead with her godmother, Lady Sarah."

Geoff knew his jaw must be hanging, for it took some effort to close it. Richard's aunt Sarah? He was fond of the old bird, in his way, but the countess of Fairbright had this habit of skewering a chap with her cane. Having shared many a youthful scrape with Richard, that walking stick had delivered more than enough punishment to his person.

"Impossible," he told his uncle. "Such an alliance cannot hope to succeed."

"Please understand." Pithnevel used a rare pleading tone. "With Napoleon on the loose again, we face a grave national crisis. It is of the utmost importance that General Drummond's mind be freed of other concerns. I would consider it a personal favor, Geoff, it you could see your way clear to take this on."

His sense of self-preservation screamed out at him to say no, *Never!* but his conscience kept reminding him that his uncle had never before begged a favor. Deuce take it, but Geoff could find no way to refuse.

"I ask only that you consider my proposal," Pithnevel pressed. "You can give me your answer in a few days' time."

"I suppose I could mull it over a bit."

"Call upon Miss Drummond. It will reassure you, I am certain. She is currently residing at her father's town house in Cavendish Square."

Geoff nodded stupidly. As his uncle bent to look at some papers, Geoff made good his escape, for heaven alone knew what else he might agree to should he stay but a minute more in the room.

Going directly to the stables, he visited his horses. His grays might be unable to offer advice, but he often sought their company when troubled. They were like family to him, those mares, but unlike others in this household, they never asked for more than he was willing to give.

A favor, his uncle had pleaded; keep Miss Drummond from harm.

"Remember the last time we tried that?" he asked the animals as he stroked their manes. He winced, thinking of the look of hurt and anger on Jeremy Wharton's face. Ten years of friendship, gone in a flash, and all because of a female's selfish whim. For two days later, before Geoff had the chance to explain or apologize, poor old Jeremy had been called up to serve with Wellington and had never returned from Spain.

"Honor Drummond is nothing but trouble," he told his horses. "If I had any sense of self-preservation, I'd hitch up the curricle and get us the devil out of town."

Yet the more he thought of how ruthlessly she had charmed him—used him—all to betray his very good friend, the more he felt he must at least pay the heartless miss a call. Today he had plans to meet his friends, but tomorrow afternoon he could stage a surprise visit. It should be diverting, if not gratifying, to see her face at the moment of recognition.

He grinned. It was nothing so base as revenge, mind you, but he rather relished the idea of watching her discomposure as she learned just who her watchdog would be.

❧ 3 ❧

Geoff stood at the door of the coffee room, somewhat loathe to enter, for it seemed no more welcoming than the three other clubs he'd been to this evening. Stale smoke, desultory talk, drab furnishings—why had he never before noticed these things?

It was all so predictable, really. Every night, Brummel could be found at his table, lecturing someone on the merits of a correctly connected cravat. Politicians argued with the less fribble-minded, while gossips flapped their tongues as they kept their ears open for the latest *on dit*.

And there in the corner sat the worst of the lot, the ever-awful Fortesque, listening intently as he munched on the inevitable joint. Insipid food and inane conversation. Was this all life had to offer?

"Geoff! You old reprobate, here you are at last."

Across the room, Jamie, Lord Bellington, bounced up from his chair. A bundle of mischief was Jamie, but a finer friend could not be found.

Unless one considered Adam, Lord Foxley, who rose as abruptly beside him, Outwardly Jamie's opposite, his lean, aristocratic features making him seem stuffier than he truly was, Adam was generally up to any prank—provided both risk and consequence were not too dear. "I say, old man," he said now with a smile, reaching to clasp Geoff's hand, "I do hope you've recovered from your, er, from last night."

Geoff's pleasure faded into embarrassment as he hazily remembered having gone on in some length about his foiled romance with Andrea Gratham. As if likewise disconcerted, both gentlemen sat quickly and offered a glass of wine.

"Have you heard the talk?" Jamie blurted as he poured.

"One wonders how you hear anything," Adam teased, "when you are the one most often spouting off."

Jamie grinned. "I'd have to be deaf not to hear that Honor Drummond has come back to town."

Geoff gripped the stem of his glass. Must all conversation of late involve that infernal female?

"Everyone who is anyone is talking about it," Jamie went on. "I say, do you remember the time she challenged Horatio Duncan to a curricle race?"

There was no sadder case than Richard's cousin. Hard to say where Horatio was most inept, in his choice of wagers, or his selection of clothes.

"Poor Horatio." Jamie laughed, proving his sympathies did not truly lie with the man. "He assumed that since she hadn't a cart to her name, how could he lose? He couldn't know she would take it into her head to steal a phaeton."

Ah, so now he could add theft to the woman's crimes.

"The way I heard it," Adam said, "Drummond granted his daughter permission to use his rig."

"He uttered that afterward, *after* he'd already sent out half his regiment to search for it."

"Yes, but he claimed it slipped his mind that he had offered it to his daughter."

Jamie gave a derisive snort. "Said that not to lose face.

Thinks the ton looks down on him as it is. And no wonder, the way Lady Sarah snubs him. A mere soldier, marrying into the exalted Fairbright clan and all that."

Geoff could sympathize with Drummond. Losing face, be he soldier or earl, was the bane of any man's existence, and he'd had troubles of his own with Miss Drummond on that score.

"Then, too," Jamie continued with a smile, "there was the incident that convinced the general to send her away."

Daunted, Geoff busied himself with refilling their glasses. He'd been convinced that none but those directly involved had known of the embarrassing affair, yet first his uncle brought it up, and now his friends. All he'd need was for Fortesque to start talking about it next.

"I never knew what actually happened. Seemed quite the hushed-up affair."

Before Geoff could relax at Adam's words, Jamie grinned ear-to-ear. Had a weakness for a good tale, did Lord Bellington, in both the hearing and the telling. "And well it should be. There were rumors—"

"Aren't there always?"

"Good point," Jamie conceded, "since in this case, the details seem somewhat farfetched. One must wonder if even Miss Drummond would dare flag down a stranger's carriage at that hour of night."

Geoff froze.

"Hard to credit indeed." Adam lifted his aquiline nose, the picture of offended taste. "What true gentleman would comply? Consider the ramifications. The chit could never show her face in London again!"

Geoff squirmed. All well and good to consider this now, but Adam and Jamie had not been drinking brandy. Nor had they been infected by a need to just once play the dashing knight.

"Alas," said a voice at Geoff's shoulder, "but that is precisely what I told Miss Drummond myself."

Geoff whirled to put face to voice and rather wished he had not. For there stood Fortesque, dressed as ever to the nines and looking altogether too pleased with himself.

The ton might find him an amiable enough fellow, but Fortesque was Geoff's proverbial thorn. From first glance, they'd been locked in competition, and whatever the skirmish, there seemed no depths too childish to which Geoff would not succumb to prove himself the better man.

"Wouldn't breathe a word of this to anyone else, of course," Fortesque went on, his eyes holding an eager gleam as he settled himself, uninvited, at the table, "but I was with Miss Drummond that night. Told me herself she'd do anything to avoid marrying old Wart."

"On this, you have started the rumor?"

Fortesque glared at Geoff, returning the antipathy in full measure. "Of course not, Stone. I—"

"You should address him as Lennox now," Adam corrected. "The *earl* of Lennox."

Fortesque ignored him. "I was there when she decided to bolt. In truth, I suggested the stunt myself." His smile drooped, as if sensing his audience was not as appreciative as he'd hoped. "Er, that is, I merely mentioned that at so late a date, her sole hope of escaping old Wart was to run away. Of course," he stumbled on when the silence stretched too long, "I hadn't been serious about our wager. I knew she hadn't a prayer of outrunning the general."

"Wager?" That vixen, Geoff thought. She had accosted him, humiliated him, all on a dare?

"The girl was forever challenging a chap," Fortesque countered belligerently, "and winning most of the time, too. Why shouldn't I take advantage of so sure a bet?"

Conscious that he'd said much the same about the wager with his cousins, Geoff insisted Miss Drummond's situation was altogether different. It was the man's place to make a challenge. And Honor Drummond could be glad she wasn't male, he thought angrily, else he'd be tempted to call her out.

Though not even she, he hoped, was outrageous enough to duel at dawn.

". . . the girl is now quite reformed," he heard Fortesque ramble on, "and means to atone for her earlier behavior."

Unable to stop himself, Geoff snorted.

"You doubt what I say, Stone?" Fortesque sat straighter in his chair, the familiar air of challenge glittering in his eyes.

Though it was Miss Drummond's ability to reform he found in doubt, Geoff was unable to resist any challenge Fortesque might pose. As such, he snorted again.

"Here, here," Adam interrupted, looking from one to the other of them. "There's no need—"

"I happen to *know* she's mended her ways," Fortesque went on, raising his weak chin in the air. "Five will give you ten that she is married before the Season is out."

Geoff shook his head. "Your odds are generous. One cannot waltz in at the tail end of the Season and snag a husband—especially not one of Miss Drummond's repute."

Fortesque leaned forward. "I am willing to put my money where *my* mouth is."

Geoff saw only the haughtiness in the man's features, not where this would lead. "Haven't you lost enough of the family fortune to my purse, Fortesque?"

"Have a care." Adam, ever aware of the properties, nodded over his shoulder to the gossips. "Ears in the wall, you know. Think of the girl's reputation. Wouldn't want the gossips carrying tales about this."

"We won't wager money then," Fortesque said with a wave of his hand, again ignoring Adam's call to caution.

"What say we wager my new rig for your curricle and pair?"

"His horses?" Jamie looked aghast. "Gads, Forty, you know he adores those animals."

"He's the one who's so sure of himself. I merely suggest that Stone stand behind his words. If he dares."

"Lennox," Geoff corrected in clipped tones. "And I think I have proven satisfactorily enough in the past that I can answer any challenge you might pose."

"Then we have a wager?"

It was at this point, and far too late, that Geoff suffered his first misgivings. "A wager it is," he said, knowing it would take a poorer sport than he to back down now. "But first, I want the conditions made clear. Miss Drummond must wed *before* the Season is over." It might be small-minded to quibble over details, but past dealings with Fortesque suggested it was wiser to leave no stones unturned.

Fortesque smirked. "I see no difficulty on that score. I'm told the Baron von Studhoff insists upon a date in June."

Geoff's first thought was that the fool was bluffing, as was his habit, but then he recalled a similarly triumphant expression on Hermione's face.

"I'm sorry, didn't I mention their engagement?" Fortesque gave him an infuriating grin. "Sorry, Stone, it must have slipped my mind."

Were his cousins also aware of Miss Drummond's marital plans? They must be, the treacherous cheats. Judging by Adam's and Jamie's embarrassed faces, Geoff must be the only one in London who had *not* known.

A smug Fortesque bid his leave, no doubt anxious to go off and boast, and Geoff left soon after. The thought of his grays in the hands of that imbecile made him too ill to eat. He was consumed by the need to see his animals safe.

Yet though he found them in good order, his anxiety did

not abate. He knew he had made a grave mistake. What could he have been thinking of, to involve himself in not one, but two ill-advised wagers? Drat that Miss Drummond; once again, it was all her fault.

He should take the job his uncle offered, he thought angrily. That way, he could use said office, not to keep Miss Drummond from trouble, but to steer her directly in its path. After all, it wouldn't be the first time scandal kept her from being married.

It occurred, fleetingly, that such an action would make him a proper cad. These wagers did not involve a meaningless race or the simple-minded pummeling of a man's features; the results could well blacken the woman's name.

Yet the more he thought about the callous manner in which she had used him—and others—the more self-righteous he grew. Deuce take it, he was not about to lose his horses.

After all, if Miss Drummond were truly as reformed as everyone claimed, she would remain immune to his efforts. And if she were not . . .

"We ain't done yet," he told his horses grimly. "We've got a good month to keep her away from that altar."

The following morning, General Drummond was wishing that altar was a good deal nearer at hand as he watched the earl of Lennox stride into the room down the hall. Pithnevel knew of Honor's upcoming marriage; one would think the general's good friend and employer would have the tact to keep his rakehell relative out of town.

Nothing must interfere with that wedding, Drummond vowed as he eased shut his office door. Pacing before his desk, he insisted Honor must wed the baron—and the sooner the better.

As if his account books stood open before him, he could

see the splashes of red. "A disaster," his man of business had decreed. "Damned near ruin."

Drummond had feared the news would be bad—and he'd tried to prepare for it—but how could anyone suspect his finances could worsen as much, or as quickly, as they had?

He stopped himself from pacing. He must not rant and rave as he was wont to do, for no one must ever guess that he had come to so uncomfortable a pass. He'd rather die in the poorhouse than admit to the snobs of London that he hadn't the acumen to handle his holdings, or the means to now climb out of debt.

And most of all, he wanted the baron kept in the dark.

For would von Studhoff be as willing to discharge Drummond's obligations once he learned their full extent? Theirs had been a gentleman's agreement, with nothing signed between them, and however much the man insisted he adored the girl ... well, suffice it to say, Drummond had his doubts that any bridegroom could be that eager.

Not that his daughter was unable to inspire adoration, he thought with a reluctant smile. All fatherly pride aside, Honor was quite a fetching thing, as beautiful as her sainted mother. How like Evelyn Honor had seemed, the day she'd agreed to the baron's suit. So fragile, so eager to please, and yet ...

He shook himself, refusing to dwell on the past. Like any competent military leader, he must keep to the matters at hand. If Honor had lowered her expressive eyes that day, who was to say her newfound docility had not caused the gesture? Since she'd returned from Scotland, she'd been as biddable a chit as any father could hope for. That nonsense she'd once spouted about love and romance was clearly outgrown and forgotten. She was ready to settle down; she had learned how to be a proper wife for the baron.

Drummond refused to admit that his fingers were crossed behind his back, or that his eyes were raised heavenward in prayer.

~4~

Gazing at the invitation list for tonight's musicale at Haversham Hall, Lady Sarah groaned. Where were the impetuous young misses to provide the diversions so prevalent in her time? Even the young bucks, once so entertaining in their exploits, seemed more apt to whine about their ennui than seek the means to combat it.

Her old friend Violet, Lady Haversham, had become the worst of the lot. Absurd, to insist that at threescore and twelve, one must grow up. "Aging gracefully," she and Amelia had the effrontery to spout, when growing senile was the far more likely term. "Be sensible," they'd tittered when Sarah complained of Honor's prospective husband. "You cannot hope for a better match."

In Sarah's opinion, it was bad enough to have a mere soldier insinuate himself into the family folds, but she would not allow Drummond to compound such ineptitude by letting that odious von Studhoff into the clan. One social mushroom per family was tragedy enough.

The only way to now rid themselves of the baron, Sarah feared, was to find someone who might supplant him. The

Who, the How, and the When, must all be handled with the utmost discretion and stealth.

The more she thought of the difficulties, the more Sarah realized she needed help. But where, in all London, would she find anyone with the necessary spirit and imagination?

As if the pair had come up to tap her shoulder, she could see the grinning Gratham twins. Remembering the part Amanda and Pandora had played in bringing their older sister and Richard together, Sarah knew that giggling twosome would be perfect for the task. If only the twins were not off with Andrea, helping her plan for her wedding.

And why could they not do their planning in town? Summon Andrea and her devoted sisters were bound to follow. One of the few advantages to being a dowager, she reasoned, was in ordering one's family about.

Chuckling, Sarah set her quill to paper. Matchmaking, scheming, manipulating others—oh, what delicious fun this Season would be.

Approaching the Drummond doorstep, Geoff found his mood to be as dark as the skies. He did not blame the threatening rain for this, but rather his visit with Lady Sarah. The gall of the woman, implying he could take a lesson or two about mending his ways from Miss Drummond.

And then to suggest—no, demand—that he escort both Miss Drummond and Lady Sarah to a night of utter boredom at Haversham Hall.

Nourishing his anger with every step, he let his impression of Miss Drummond grow from a spoiled young miss into a veritable dragon. He could remember little of her from their brief encounter, so it was quite easy to convince himself that she could not have much in the way of looks or manner to commend her. Else why had she settled for the shy, retiring Wart? She must be a managing sort of female, Geoff decided, a bully of the first order, with a face that could stop a clock.

So feeling, he knocked upon her door, confident that he had the element of surprise on his side. Yet as these things too often happen, it was Geoff instead who found himself at a loss for words.

He was admitted cordially enough by her butler, but it was not in some cozy drawing room that the confounded female greeted him, but rather in the hallway, as she came bounding forward in pursuit of a rather large and very wet dog.

"Stop!" she called out, swiping damp blonde curls from her eyes.

Geoff had occasion to note the dog was a great golden oaf of a thing, with features like his cousin Iris and a pedigree too questionable to mention. It did not so much as flinch as its mistress threatened its life, but rather bowled past out the door, which caused Miss Drummond, in her blind panic to overtake it, to tumble right into Geoff's unprepared arms.

To his chagrin, those arms wrapped around Miss Drummond protectively and it was far from the unpleasant experience he wanted it to be. For far too long a pause, he merely stood there, gazing into her eyes, and wondering how it would feel to kiss her silly.

"My dog," she said suddenly, regaining wits enough to break away. "I must fetch him."

"Not dressed like that, I pray."

Her hands clasped her wet wrapper, which was no doubt meant to protect the sodden—and badly torn—morning gown underneath. "Oh my, yes. But what can I do? My dog . . . the general . . . he'll kill us both . . . I must . . ."

"I'll fetch the dog," Geoff found himself offering, albeit

ungraciously. And her smile of relief gave him no choice
but to take off down the street.

He had no difficulty locating the beast; the shrieks of
each lady it passed—and shook itself off upon—made a
more than reliable trail. Geoff chose to think his coaxings
about a possible meal convinced the mongrel to take itself
home, but it was more likely the rain, making good on its
threat of the past two days.

Trotting behind the dog, just as wet and twice as dis-
gruntled, Geoff belatedly realized he might better have let
its mistress go after it. Think of the talk she would gener-
ate should she be caught wondering the streets in such dis-
habille. It might even scare off her baron.

Geoff could have won both his wagers then, and without
spending a single day in her company.

Confound it, what was there about the chit that had him
ever playing the gallant, when a wiser man would flee for
his life?

She waited at the door, looking more lovely than she
had any right to be. Though still slightly damp, her golden
curls cascaded from a knot at the top of her head, with a
few strategically escaped ringlets framing her flushed
cheeks. Chin-high and long-sleeved, the pale pink morning
gown she now wore concealed her neck and shoulders, but
while the earlier view might be gone, it was not—to
Geoff's chagrin—entirely forgotten.

"You've found him!" she gushed as if he had offered
the moon. "How can I ever repay you?"

Disconcerted by her warm welcome, Geoff nearly
blurted that damsels in distress customarily offered a kiss,
but he remembered in time that he was there to provoke
her into bad behavior, not indulge in it himself.

Besides, he was quite disgustingly damp at the moment.
A fact she seemed to recognize at the same time.

"Please, you must come in and warm yourself by the

fire. I'll ring for hot tea. Oh, and Rawlings!" she added over her shoulder. "We'll need some brandy as well."

Few young ladies would think to offer a caller such restoring spirits. As there was nothing he'd like more at the moment, Geoff found himself unbending.

She ushered him into the drawing room, apparently unaware that the dog had followed until it tried to settle itself on the sofa. "Oh no, you don't," she admonished, pulling at its collar. "Do you wish the general to shoot you here and now?"

"I daresay he would at least march the dog outside, miss," offered a dry voice behind them.

"Indeed, Rawlings?" Miss Drummond grinned. "Have you forgotten the shambles the general made of the library back at Drummond House? We spent nearly a week picking the shells out of the walls."

"Quite so." The butler frowned at the dog. "I imagine you wish me to take him back to the kitchen?"

"Please, and do finish his bath." Dragging the dog by its collar, she gave it over into the butler's grasp. "I hate to impose, but Lolly must be made ready. Just in case."

Both mistress and butler looked expectantly to Geoff. Miss Drummond was smiling; Rawlings was not.

"Lolly?" was all Geoff could think of to say.

She laughed delightfully. "His head has this way of lolling whenever he's in a scold. Though I assure you, it is not all that often," she hastily added. "He just needs the room to romp a bit. The country would be ideal."

As Rawlings stumbled off with the animal, a maid entered with a tray. Pouring Geoff's brandy, she went to a chair in the corner. A chaperon? Geoff wondered distractedly, or a guard? Looking to his hostess, he suspected that all this was leading somewhere, but he could not for the life of him determine where.

Miss Drummond gestured him to the sofa. "Indeed, the

general would not have been bent upon his destruction if
Lolly wasn't forever ingratiating himself with his prized
greyhounds. There was a litter, you see . . ." She shook her
head sadly. "That was when the general took after Lolly
with his shotgun."

She has dimples, Geoff marvelled as he took his seat on
the sofa. And, he realized with a start, she was waiting for
him to speak. "Your father must have dreadful aim."

"The general is a crack shot," she said with blatant
pride. "Had Lolly not raced with the wind, the general
would no doubt have done a good deal more than just nick
him on the leg. Thank heavens the wound left a bloody
enough trail, though. When the general assumed Lolly was
dead, we saw no reason to disillusion him."

Geoff didn't want to smile, but he couldn't seem to stop
himself.

She took the seat opposite and began pouring tea. "You
mustn't think Lolly is a complete scamp," she went on.
"Why, my aunt never even knew he came to Scotland."
She frowned, as if she found the memory an unpleasant
one, before resuming in a wistful tone. "Granted, he spent
a good deal of his time running wild over the moors. Had
a proper spree, Lolly did. Many was the time I sorely en-
vied him."

With a sigh, she clasped her hands in her lap. "But so
much has changed for us both. I'd be a wretch to keep him
now. Even without my father's antipathy, London is no
place for a dog like Lolly."

"I should say not." Geoff rather wondered if there was
any place suitable for the beast.

Miss Drummond beamed. "I knew you'd agree. Deep
down, he's a good boy. As loyal as the day is long. And
just wait until you see how grand he looks after his bath,
with his coat brushed and glistening. You shan't regret
this, I promise."

"I beg your pardon?"

"Lolly. When he comes to live with you."

This was what she'd been leading toward? Geoff could only stare, astounded by her gall. Did she think that merely because he'd been foolish enough to come to her rescue once, he was gap-skulled enough to do so again?

"Of course, I shall want to know a bit more about you before I can let him go. Lolly is more than a pet to me, you must understand; he is like family. Before I can let you have him, I would like to know more about your own relations, where your estate is situated—that sort of thing."

"Let me have him? My dear Miss Drummond, just who do you take me for, that you can believe I will now take on the care of your dog?"

She eyed him with undisguised alarm. "You're not Mr. Jackson-Smythe?"

Irked that she had failed to recognize him—had not even known he was Quality—Geoff summoned depths of arrogance he had not known he owned. "Indeed I am not. The name's Lennox."

"Oh my, not the *earl* of Lennox? But of course, Lady Sarah warned you might come . . . I quite forgot, what with Mr. Jackson-Smythe . . . oh my heavens, the way I've rattled on—what a pea goose you must think me."

It was hard not to take pity, for she seemed so confused. But Geoff had responded to her helplessness once before, and just look where that had led him.

Setting down his brandy, he rose to his feet. "Do forgive me, but I've urgent matters requiring my attention. I fear I must go."

"You can't mean to leave?" she said, rising just as quickly beside him. "Why, you haven't even tasted your tea."

He looked down his nose, refusing to be charmed. Her dismay stemmed less from the loss of his company, he didn't doubt, than the fear she might lose the chance to rid herself of an unruly pet. "My purpose in coming here is duty, not pleasure," he said, being his most priggish. "Lady Sarah has bid me inform you that I am to escort you both to tonight's entertainment at Haversham Hall. She seems to feel I shall be a steadying influence, there to fend off any trouble you might otherwise find."

"I see," she said stiffly, but he thought he saw a flash of rebellion in those remarkably green eyes. The deep breath proved she was no more immune to his jibes than Iris or Hermione. Could she, too, be induced to do something positively outrageous just to spite him?

Daring her to do so, Geoff turned on a heel, though he paused at the door to deliver a parting shot. "Oh, and do try to be ready by nine. There's nothing more loathsome, I find, than a female who keeps a man waiting."

He was quite certain she huffed as he sailed out of the room. Splendid. By the time he arrived tonight—not until well past ten—he'd have her seething. One skillfully placed taunt, and she'd do most anything to defy him.

He hesitated, remembering her face as she'd talked about her ridiculous dog, but he quickly suppressed all misgivings. She'd thought him a common farmer, he must not forget. Not only treated him like a nobody, but regarded him as one as well.

It was only fair, he insisted stubbornly, that he goad her into some minor indiscretion. Causing the baron to cry off was the only way to keep his horses.

And considering that mutinous look in her eyes, making Miss Drummond misbehave should be child's play.

In truth, mutiny was the farthest thing from Honor's mind. With something close to despair, she wondered how she would survive the evening ahead. Making Society accept her had seemed quite some task before, but now, with

Lennox set upon being difficult, it seemed near impossible.

She could have told Lady Sarah an earl would want nothing to do with her, but even without the cane, her godmother had always frightened her speechless. In the end, Honor had agreed to wait and at least meet the man. She was not so lost to Society's ways that she failed to see the merits in having an earl seem to dangle after her, how his name and position could ease her way back into the ton.

She swallowed, hard. How she dreaded tonight; no one knew better how the gossips could be. Indeed, she'd happily abandon the project, had she not promised her father she'd reinstate their good name.

"Begging your pardon, miss, but will you be wanting me to take the tray now?"

Honor looked up in surprise, having forgotten Betsy was in the room. How like her maid to anticipate the need for chaperonage, but then, it seemed her servants were always there to protect her. Smiling, Honor told the girl to please take the tray to the kitchen.

Betsy gave Honor a freckled grin. "Don't you be minding his lordship, miss. Men don't like to admit when they've taken a fancy, but mark my words, he'll soon be eating the crumbs from your hands. You could charm the devil himself, you know."

What nonsense, Honor thought as Betsy left the room, but she could not still the flush creeping over her face. Taken a fancy? What could Betsy have seen that she had not?

She reddened, remembering that all-too-brief moment in his arms. How strong he had seemed, how tall and protective. And there had been a delicious moment, gazing up into those soft gray eyes, when she'd thought—or hoped?—that their lips might actually meet.

But his subsequent abruptness merely brought home

how little she knew about the ways of the ton. Appearance was all, she'd been told, and yet she'd been so busy gazing at his auburn hair and lurking grin, she had never even noticed the cut of his clothes.

Talking that way to him, an earl—my heavens, what he must think of her now.

No, Betsy must be wrong. Not that it would matter, in any case. She was engaged to be married, bound by the wishes of her intended, and she was not about to have her head turned by some absurdly handsome earl. However much she might long to tell von Studhoff to jump off London Bridge, she would keep her word to her father.

But as she trudged upstairs to her room, she could not help but think of the few times Lennox had grinned back at her. Something had clicked into place from the first moment she'd seen the man, and it had been so remarkably easy to talk to him.

If only she could make Lennox feel as comfortable in her presence as she'd felt in his. Going out upon the town would be far less daunting if she had an ally in the ton, a rock to cling to when the sharks of London came looking for her blood.

And tonight, she thought with a gulp, they'd be out in full force.

$$\approx 5 \approx$$

Whistling as he strode to the door, Geoff consulted his watch. He was pleased to note it was considerably past ten. Grinning broadly, he pictured Miss Drummond pacing in a snit abovestairs, her calculated entrance stalled, her intricate coiffure beginning to wilt.

But barely had he raised his hand to knock, when the door swung open, and there stood Honor Drummond before him.

She was draped in gray from neck to foot, with nary a gem to add light to her person. Pulled back in a severe knot, her golden hair was disguised by a fine dusting of powder. All limbs were likewise concealed behind an inordinate waste of silk, wrought in a design that could not be more matronly, and with an effect so unappealingly lifeless, Miss Drummond could have been one of the marble statues posing in the hall.

Until a timid smile flashed into brilliance, and her green eyes warmed with welcome.

Silly chit, Geoff thought, trying his best not to react to that smile. Didn't she know it was in bad taste to open one's own door? And deuce take it, she shouldn't be beaming at him; she should be whining.

In the interest of good manners, he offered to help with her cape, but he refused to fabricate any compliments about her appearance. "You must have misheard me," he said irritably. "I mentioned a musicale, not a funeral."

There was a second's hesitation as her smile faded away, but she offered no other response. "I must dress to please my intended," she said, ignoring his offer and donning the cape herself. "The baron requests I wear more muted colors."

Geoff considered this utter rot; he was certain she'd dressed thus to defy him. "And just where is the baron," he asked, "that he does not escort you and your godmother tonight? For that matter, where is Lady Sarah?"

"The baron might join us later. As for my—"

On cue, Lady Sarah appeared in the hallway. "What kept you, Lennox?" she barked as he helped her with her cape. "Been dallying again in your club? I was about to return home, certain you meant not to show."

Her words did nothing to improve Geoff's mood. Though he'd like nothing better than to turn tail and hie off to White's, he could have hoped Lady Sarah would realize he was not cad enough to indulge himself so. That having committed himself to this wretched evening, he'd feel compelled to see it through to the end.

"Likely did us a favor, though," Lady Sarah continued to grumble as he settled them into his coach. "With luck, we'll have missed most of the caterwauling by the time we arrive. Can't abide Violet's singing; never could."

A slim hope, dashed the instant they entered Haversham Hall. Gushing as she led them to the music room, Lady Violet announced that the entertainment had been held back for their arrival. How could she begin without her "dearest Sarah"?

Herded about the room, presented to people he'd avoided for years, Geoff realized that the delay—indeed, the whole evening—had been orchestrated for Miss Drummond's sake. Yet while Lady Haversham might have acted with good intent, there was a fishbowl quality to the attention her guest of honor received. All those curious, and often rude stares—Miss Drummond must feel as if she'd sprouted a wart on her nose. As she seemed to shrivel before his eyes, Geoff was hard-pressed to remember that she deserved much worse.

And the "worse" came as they sat, and were forced to endure the musical renditions of Lady Violet and her less-than-gifted friends. Although oddly enough, Miss Drummond seemed to enjoy the performance. When the program ended, she peeled off her gloves to give volume to her enthusiastic response. "I adore music," she explained when Geoff looked at her in amazement.

"My dear girl, that was not music. It was torture, as any trained ear can tell you."

Her hands stilled in her lap, looking rather helpless there. "You are no doubt right," she said in a small voice. "It's just that it's been so long since I've taken part in any entertainment. I suppose I quite lost my head." She looked around them, reddening as she noticed that the applause was nominal at best.

"Go easy on her," Lady Sarah said in her penetrating tone. "Can't you see the chit is nervous enough this first night out?"

Though her mark had been Geoff, the barb missed its target, for it was Miss Drummond who shrank in her chair. Seeing this, Geoff was left wondering if the chit had donned all the gray, not to spite him as he had let himself suppose, but rather to avoid the public eye.

"I suppose I must pay my regards to Amelia," Lady Sarah grumbled as she rose to her feet. Glancing back at the door, she added. "Take care of my goddaughter in my absence. I daresay she will need your support."

Clearly perplexed, Miss Drummond glanced over her shoulder. She straightened—went quite stiff, actually—and gasped, "Oh dear, the baron."

Geoff too looked back, as did all else in the room. Such attention did not escape the baron's notice, Geoff saw. Indeed, the man seemed to puff up to twice his considerable girth as spine erect, his bald dome gleaming a good head or two above the other gentlemen, von Studhoff marched forward.

His apparel, almost foppish in its leanings toward pink and gold, was crafted of the finest silks and satins. Gems glittered with reckless abandon, on his hands, cuffs, and towering shirt points. Partaking freely from a gold-encrusted snuffbox as he joined them, the man made it clear that pampering himself was his favorite occupation.

Geoff rose to greet the man for courtesy sake, but he had a peculiar urge to stay close to Miss Drummond.

Reeking of condescension, von Studhoff nodded briefly at the introductions, before turning to his bride-to-be. "You are dressed more sensibly this time," he began in a crisp German accent. "But where is your wig? Have we not discussed the vanity in showing off your hair?"

"I-I powdered it."

What was the baron about? Geoff wondered. Even a foreigner must know wigs had long since gone out of fashion.

"And where are your gloves?" the man went on. "Your father assured me, after I generously offered my name, that you would be more mindful of the proprieties."

Miss Drummond looked down at her chair where the errant gloves rested, and promptly, if reluctantly, replaced them on her hands.

Geoff bristled. He—of all people—might know there

were aspects of her behavior that begged for improvement, but where was the need for public harping?

As he thought this, Miss Drummond chanced to look up. Seeing again the flash of rebellion in her green eyes, Geoff realized why she so meekly lowered them. Were the baron to see the loathing there, he'd likely freeze on the spot.

He found himself smiling, for whatever his own peeves against the girl, Geoff could not like to see her knuckle under to such a prig. Perhaps that was why, when her gaze met his, he gave in to the absurd impulse to wink.

She blinked twice, as if to focus, and then a swift grin came to those soft, full lips.

"You smile at this?" the baron asked. "My dear girl, this is hardly a matter for levity."

Miss Drummond promptly lowered her eyes again, schooling her features into a model of female decorum. Oddly disturbed by this, Geoff did not at first hear von Studhoff announce that he needn't trouble himself over escorting Miss Drummond home. The baron had to repeat the statement, adding that he would see to the duty himself. Although Lennox, if he would be so kind, could see Lady Sarah back to her town house.

Thus trapped, Geoff had to choice but to escort said lady home, though he did so in forbidding silence. Being who she was, of course, the old harpy could not fail to comment upon it.

Though she did wait until they were at her doorstep, no doubt hoping to maximize the sting. "Never fear," Lady Sarah soothed, patting his arm. "Any fool can see you and the girl are made for each other."

"I beg your pardon?"

"I bet you a farthing you'll marry her in the end."

"I must talk with Richard about you." Geoff shook his head. "Your nephew needs to know you're turning senile."

She cackled, for this was the sort of banter on which she thrived. "A farthing, my boy, and don't you forget it." She went through the door, then turned to face him. "I say, what are you going to do about that lout, von Studhoff?"

"You know the adage about making one's bed," he told her stiffly, turning to leave. "Far be it for me to rob that female of her just reward."

"Rubbish!" he heard her throw out as he turned to go. "You won't leave her in his clutches. You must act, boy, and act quickly. I cannot like the look in that devil's eye."

A sentiment Honor herself shared as she bid farewell to the man she seemed more and more doomed to marry. She tried not to shudder as the baron bent down to kiss her hand, but how could she not? She was committed to a lifetime of this.

Watching the baron march out the door, she thought what an utter disaster the night had been. Society's matrons would never invite her back into their ranks, not when her intended did his best to expose her faults.

Making her way to her bedroom, she realized she should have said something to the general, that first night she'd met von Studhoff, for she'd known at once that they would never suit. Each time she thought of his first kiss— that sloppy assault on her mouth—she had an overpowering urge to again run away.

She entered her room, the sole light coming from the dying blaze, its logs giving off one last, protesting hiss. As she lit a candle, Honor felt a great empathy with that fire, feeling the same need to fight her fate, yet knowing it was a lost cause. She was no longer a feckless, heedless child. Having given her word, she was now bound to this marriage, trapped as effectively as her hands were within these hateful gloves.

Cover your hands, the baron forever harped, but what he truly expected was that Honor would bury her soul.

Remembering his kiss on her hand, she wrenched off the gloves and flung them to the floor. Heaven help her, how was she to marry a man whose very touch filled her with disgust?

Sitting on the bed, she brought her fingers to her lips, thinking of another kiss—one so deliciously anticipated, yet never received. This morning, bumping into him, she had not recoiled from the earl's touch. If anything, she had wanted it overmuch.

Blushing profusely, she wondered if perhaps the baron was right, and she truly did require moral guidance.

Somewhat chastened, she reached for the gloves, but her fingers refused to close over them. All at once, it was not the baron she suddenly saw in her mind, but rather Lennox and his audacious wink.

At first, she had blamed her imagination, but then he had grinned with a hint of conspiracy. Had he alone seen her rebellion? Had he meant to encourage it?

She pulled her hands back to her lap, leaving the gloves where they were. She was not by nature the glum sort, nor inclined to accept life's unpleasantries if there were a way to change them. There were always alternatives, she'd always believed, and wasn't now the time to find one?

After all, if the general merely wished her wed and safely off his hands, did the actual candidate matter? If his fondest wish was to be accepted by the ton, an earl could accomplish this feat as well as—if not better—than a baron.

She would need to think on this, of course; indeed, the idea would require careful scrutiny.

In the meantime, however, she kicked the gloves under her bed.

* * *

Unable to sleep, Geoff continued to ponder over Lady Sarah's words. What on earth could he have said or done to prompt the old crone to suggest marriage? And to Honor Drummond, of all people.

Uneasily, he remembered that wink.

Deuce take it, what was a man to do? Let the poor girl wilt under the barrage of the baron's abuse? Granted, Miss Drummond no longer seemed quite as awful as he'd once believed, but matrimony? Lady Sarah was far off the mark. This was one wager he would win hands down.

Yet the more he considered the suggestion, the less ideal his own plan seemed. Making Miss Drummond misbehave now seemed uncomfortably knavish. It would take a hardened cad to tarnish her already dubious name.

What an inappropriate time for his conscience to introduce itself, he grumbled as he punched his pillow into a more comfortable form. All well and good to act the gentleman, but must it cost him his horses? There must be some way to stop the dratted female's wedding—short of participating in one himself.

Short of participating, he repeated, his eyes opening wide. But of course, why couldn't *he* court the woman? Not that he'd actually marry her, but there could be no harm in a little flirtation. He need merely instill sufficient doubt about the baron as an adequate choice to deflect her current plans, and then he could cut himself loose. Indeed, when one considered the way von Studhoff treated Miss Drummond, Geoff would actually be doing the woman a favor.

Lying back on the pillow, he gave himself a mental pat on the back. It was a splendid solution and he would begin his new strategy at once.

Perhaps he would pay a call upon Miss Drummond in the morning.

~6~

Honor made her way down to breakfast, wondering how best to approach the general. There must be some way to suggest that von Studhoff might not be the ideal son-in-law, that they just might find Lennox a better prospect. She could not compare their incomes, since she'd no idea what either man was worth, nor could she assure the general that Lennox would even offer for her hand.

Oh, but she wished he would. That wink went a long way toward proving Lennox had a sense of humor, a trait she considered necessary in life and one of which her current fiancé seemed woefully devoid. Unfortunately, however, wit was not high on the general's list of husbandly assets.

Finding her father at the table, already buried in his paper, Honor nearly lost heart. Most days she was invisible to him, but when he had a newspaper to hide behind, she ceased to exist at all.

"Hmmph!" he said suddenly, causing her to start as she took her seat. "Nothing in here about the Corsican. Dratted editor is more concerned with the Regent's wardrobe than the peril of having a maniac tearing across the Continent."

Another might assume a comment was called for, but since the general believed girls were meant to be neither seen nor heard, Honor buttered a slice of toast. He was a busy man, she'd oft told herself, a hero to his country.

Yet there were times when even a daughter had need of advice and encouragement, and it always managed to hurt that the general remained too busy to spare a moment for her.

"Appears Fairbright's coming to town," he said, finding something of interest in Society's doings after all. "Jolly good soldier, Richard."

A man's exploits on the battlefield meant all to him and many was the time Honor had rued the fact that she too could not march off to war. "Hmmph," he repeated. "Says he's found himself a bride. One of Gerry Gratham's brood. Good mixture there."

Gratham had been a "jolly good soldier," too. No doubt the general was imagining Richard's future offspring emerging into the world complete with uniform and sword. Too bad Lennox had spent no time in the military; it might make persuading her father a simpler affair.

"Wedding's to take place at the end of the month," he muttered. "Wonder if we've gotten an invitation?"

He was notorious for his unopened mail; the card might yet lie on his desk. Honor hoped so, for she'd like nothing better than to witness dear Richard exchanging his vows.

Five years ago, she might have run weeping from the room at such news, but time had done much to put her infatuation in perspective. Richard had been nice to her at his aunt's request; he'd had no idea how the young and impressionable Honor, having no other role model, would soak up his words like a sponge.

When she'd asked why the ton ignored her, he'd suggested watching others to learn how to go about. "Half the room is aping someone," he'd explained with a grin. "When you haven't the knack yourself, you simply imitate the masters."

And in her limited experience, no one had ever seemed more masterful than Richard. She knew now that she might better have chosen a female model, but at the time, he had been her bright, glittering star. She'd felt certain that if she could reach out and touch but a bit of his brilliance, she too could find love and adoration wherever she went.

But there were different rules for her sex, she'd since learned. Where Richard's gambling amused the ton, her own brought disaster. Male antics might lead to fame and fortune but hers invariably led to marriage with men like the baron.

"Sir," she began slowly. "I need to speak with you."

The general frowned at her over his paper.

"I've given my marriage a good deal of thought. The baron is so . . . so Bavarian. I don't see how we can ever suit."

The general said nothing—he had no need to. The glare from his dark eyes was quite enough.

"Can't you see? I-I don't love him."

There was a tic over his right eye, but still he said nothing. Honor wriggled in her chair, feeling like a child again as she suffered through one of his inspections.

"Please try to understand," she plodded on, feeling as if she were in ten solid inches of mud. "The man makes me . . . uneasy. I shudder whenever he enters the room. I know you wish me married off, but mightn't we look elsewhere?"

"And be thought some witless here-and-therians? What's wrong with you, girl? We can't be caught crying off twice."

"The baron can make the announcement. I don't care."

"Don't care?" His skin took on a purplish hue. "Ruin, that's what we'd face. You can't play high and loose and hope to be accepted by the ton. What are you trying to do, drive me to an early grave?"

And all at once, she could see the lines in her father's face. In five years, he seemed to have aged thirty, and each new wrinkle had become an accusation, visual proof of how her past exploits had taken their toll. *If the general should die,* she thought with a jolt, *I'll have spent my entire life never knowing his love at all.*

As she tried to swallow the unwieldy lump in her throat, she heard Rawlings clearing his own at the far end of the room. "If you will pardon me, sir ... miss ... the baron von Studhoff waits without. He is most adamant about speaking with you."

The general waved absentmindedly. As if taking this for approval, Rawlings quickly withdrew from the room. Shaking his head, muttering to himself, the general settled back down in his chair, mere seconds before von Studhoff appeared at the door.

With an arrogant lack of speed, as if he'd no notion that it took a total boor to appear uninvited at such an hour, the baron strolled to Honor's side. Clicking his heels at her father, he leaned down to peck at her hand. As she still held her toast in it, a small glob of jam dripped onto his snow-white glove. Honor battled a grin, for his precise movements as he mopped the spot with his silk handkerchief warned that the baron was not nearly as amused.

"You are here early this morning," she said sugar-sweetly. She dared not add what a feat that was; it was rumored the baron rarely finished his toilette before noon.

"General, I have good news." He turned pointedly in her father's direction. "But I would not bore Honoria with our talk. Perhaps she can seek entertainment elsewhere?"

The general, who had been looking at the baron with undisguised alarm, turned swiftly to Honor, no doubt to forestall any protest hovering on her lips. "Run along, child. The baron and I, er, wish to be alone."

"But I haven't finished my breakfast!"

"I think it is as well, my beloved. You will wish to fit into your bridal gown, will you not?"

"Be a good girl now and leave us to our talk," the general said hastily, apparently blind to the fact that her "beloved" had just insulted her.

But as it was less an order and more a question—as close to a plea as the general was likely to get—Honor swallowed her rejoinder and stomped from the room.

Out in the hallway, though, she paused to stick out her tongue. Fit into her gown, indeed! The man had said that so he might finish her meal in her stead.

The general, as oblivious as he could be, must be made to see that she could not possibly spend her life with von Studhoff. Hands on her hips, she stared at the front door, willing the bell to chime. Please, Lady Sarah, she prayed silently; send Lennox to visit again this morning.

She frowned, remembering how he'd glared on his last visit. How could she offer him as an alternative to her father? Aside from that single wink, she could not safely assume that Lennox liked her any more than the baron did.

If only she knew how to charm a man. With no real skill at flirtation, how could she hope to bring Lennox up to scratch?

"Imitate the masters," Richard had advised.

Perhaps she should watch the young belles for a while, see how they handled their eager swains. She was a quick study; she should be able to find the knack soon enough.

Glancing at the door, she hastily amended her prayer. In all, it might be best if Lennox put in his appearance later in the week.

* * *

The general was more concerned with his current visitor. Eyeing von Studhoff as he settled down before the plate his daughter so recently abandoned, the general fretted over how much the man had overheard. For were he to cry off now, Drummond's financial goose would be good and truly cooked.

But von Studhoff seemed amiable enough. "I have come to tell you I have found the bitch you seek," he explained, helping himself to a generous portion of coddled eggs. "If you wish, we can go see her today."

It took some minutes for Drummond to sort through this. But then, greyhounds had to be the last thing on his mind.

"I must say, Drummond, you don't look enthused. You are still interested in rebuilding your kennels, are you not?"

"Er, yes." Unnerving, that the baron should know of his efforts in that quarter. "I am indeed, but we have discussed my financial embarrassment. You know I can ill afford to buy anything at the moment."

Von Studhoff smiled. "Ah, but my dear man, I have explained that you need never again concern yourself with the nasty business of money. Not when I, your son-to-be, am here to foot the bills. This bitch shall be my gift."

It seemed too good to be true, that the general could at long last rebuild his kennels. And all because of the baron's thoughtful gesture.

So much for Honor's protestations that they would never suit.

Thinking of how far the baron's generosity might yet extend, Drummond insisted his daughter's protests were bridal nerves. It wasn't the first time she'd had them; look at Wharton. Girls were silly creatures—utterly useless on the battlefield—so why deny himself his litter? After all, he must not forget it was Honor's mongrel that had soured, and eventually forced him to disband his original pack.

Why should he wallow in debt, merely because the chit did not yet know her own mind?

Before Drummond could answer, the doorbell gonged. Cocking his head, von Studhoff stood abruptly and went to the door to peek through it. With a brief, mumbled, "We can discuss this later," he quit the room.

Drummond stared at where he had been, never before having seen the baron moved to such speed. He wondered if this unseen caller could be a rival. His girl could be a taking thing, he thought with fatherly pride; she hadn't a worry about fitting into her bridal gown as far as he could see. A competitor—though one with no real hope of success, of course—might be the very thing to make von Studhoff all the more eager to wed her.

Satisfied, the general reached for his paper. Leave things alone, he'd always felt, and things eventually sorted themselves out.

Geoff was not nearly as complacent as he made his way to the door. By the time he rang the bell, he began to feel that making plans to court Miss Drummond was far less complicated than actually carrying them out.

Nor did it help to find von Studhoff there before him.

He emerged from a distant doorway as Geoff handed the butler his hat. Striding briskly forward, the baron sailed past Miss Drummond as if she were not there. Indeed, swathed as she was in shadow, Geoff too might have failed to notice the woman, had her smile not turned to instant dismay as the baron appeared. For Geoff, it was rather as if someone had doused the only candle in the place.

"I would ask you to come in," von Studhoff said curtly, "but alas, we are about to go out."

"Out?" Miss Drummond barely managed to squeak.

The baron whirled, quickly rearranging his features into delighted surprise. "Ah, my beloved, here you are. You are ready to leave, I hope?"

"I-I . . ."

Not waiting for her answer, he turned back to Geoff with an equally insincere smile. "A shame your trip is wasted, Lennox. Perhaps another time?"

"Actually, I hadn't meant to stay. I came merely to inquire about the time I am to escort Miss Drummond to the Makepeace Ball this evening."

"Forgetful child, did you not tell him?" Von Studhoff shook his head. "Ach, these English girls, how they scatter their thoughts. She was to tell you *I* mean to escort her this evening. There is no need to trouble yourself at all."

Geoff's gaze went to Miss Drummond. Stubbornly refusing to look his way, she kept starting at her dratted hands, as if she could read something of import upon their surface.

Rawlings smiled sympathetically as he returned Geoff's hat. With a bow in his mistress's direction, the butler made his way to the back of the house.

"Go fetch your gloves, my dear," the baron barked at Miss Drummond. "We must commence our walk."

"Walk?"

It was a poor choice of words, timed as it was with Rawlings's entrance into the kitchen. Plainly taking the question as an invitation, Lolly charged down the hallway with twice the enthusiasm of the day before.

As it jumped on Miss Drummond and proceeded to lick her face, Geoff watched in fascination. Most females would have treated them to a fit of hysterics, but she merely laughed as she tousled the animal's head.

"Filthy beast!" the baron exclaimed as he stepped forward to extricate the dog. Lolly, seeing this as a threat to its mistress, gave a low, warning growl.

Muttering angrily, von Studhoff drew back an arm to strike it, but one quick leap had the baron on the floor, with Lolly poised triumphantly on his chest. There was no licking this time, but rather a healthy display of teeth.

Between the dog's antics and all that German sputtering, Geoff was hard put not to chuckle—until he looked up to see the panic in Miss Drummond's eyes. Confound it, she couldn't expect him to make a habit of these rescues?

"Come, Lolly," he nonetheless said as he yanked on the dog's collar. "I do believe the baron prefers to stand."

"Vile, filthy creature!" Rising with wounded dignity—and no little outrage—von Studhoff brushed at his trousers. "Rest assured, Honoria, your father shall hear of this. I doubt he'd want a mongrel anywhere near his new greyhound."

"A new greyhound?" Her eyes widened all the more. "Oh, but you must not tell my father about this!"

"You would tell me what I can or cannot do?"

As she took an unconscious step backward, Geoff took one closer. "Just one moment, von Studhoff. Miss Drummond is trying to explain that, er, she's done me a favor. Been helping with old Lolly here. As you can see, it requires a bath, and I need room in which to give it one, and, well, I was somewhat wary of asking my uncle for the use of the Pithnevel kitchens."

"Are you saying this wretched animal belongs to you?"

"I fear so." Never had a phrase been so aptly used, for it did not escape Geoff's notice that this time gallantry had taken him a step too far. He could not hope Miss Drummond would refute his claim; she could not look more relieved.

"Then take your cur from my sight at once. And see

that you do not abuse my intended's generosity in the future. I know I can speak for the general when I say we will not tolerate strange animals in this home."

Lolly began to snarl again. Rather than risk another confrontation, Geoff pulled at its collar and took his leave. There was little hope the dog would refuse to go with him; the prospect of the promised walk plainly outweighed any prior loyalty. Indeed, the confounded mutt trotted off at Geoff's side as if it had always belonged there.

Looking back, hoping for at least a smile, Geoff found her eyes once more cast down in that annoyingly meek pose. Nor did she glance up as the door was shut in Geoff's face.

He must stop expecting gratitude from the chit, he told himself sternly. She simply was not capable of it.

As he hopped into his curricle, the dog settled beside him. Perched like the queen mother, gazing with interest at all they passed, it wagged its tail with such contagious enthusiasm, Geoff's hand reached out to pat its head.

"My, my, Lennox, never say *you've* got yourself a dog?" Fortesque, tooling past, did little to hide his amusement. That gazetted gossip would soon have the ton tittering that Lennox had gone soft in the heart—if not head.

And how could he refute this? Drat that Miss Drummond and her various rescues. Once again, she had done serious damage to the image he'd so carefully cultivated over the years. Hard to remain urbane and unflappable with this confounded mongrel licking one's face.

Courting her, however frivolously, might prove far more perilous than he'd thought. Just what might she need of him next?

~7~

Tucking her head back inside the window of Lady Sarah's barouche, Pandora Gratham spoke to her twin. "I believe you're right," she said with an irrepressible grin. "The baron did go into that seedy-looking tavern. Should we follow him inside?"

Amanda, by far the more cautious twin, betrayed her misgivings with a frown. "I think we must take this to Lady Sarah. I doubt she'd want us to venture into this part of town. It was altogether too bad of you to insist that poor Tom drive us here. He's likely to lose his post."

"Pooh, you worry overmuch. Didn't Lady Sarah say we were to be her ears and eyes?"

"I rather think she meant us to watch Miss Drummond," Amanda said. "And besides, the baron makes me uneasy."

Pandora understood what her sister meant. For the life of her, she could not see how Miss Drummond could marry that man. Pandora felt it her solemn duty to prove how wrong the baron was for Honor, even if it meant following him into the depths of hell. Especially if she might then see the seamier—and far more interesting—sites of London.

"We should be getting back," Amanda gently reminded. "We must dress for the Makepeace Ball."

Remembering that Lord Bellington meant to attend the affair, Pandora decided the baron could be watched as easily from a dance floor. Indeed, if they kept him busy enough, Honor would be able to talk and dance with other men.

Her eyes began to twinkle. After all, their dear, lonely Geoffrey would be there tonight.

"Must we do this?" the baron's informant whispered across the table, though no one could overhear in this din.

The baron frowned. "I've explained it in length to you."

"Of course," the man hastily added, looking down, "you must know what you're doing."

How typically British. They might boast and swagger but they were invariably cowed by the show of Teutonic might. Ach, but he longed for the day this "island of shopkeepers" was brought to its knees.

"I, er, didn't mean it the way it sounded, Baron. I was concerned, you see. Girl's known to have a temper. Wouldn't want her crying off, would we?"

Von Studhoff treated the statement with the scorn it deserved. Drummond would never let his daughter change her mind, not if he hoped to prevent his financial demise.

"Of course, Drummond would never allow it," the fool chuckled nervously as he echoed the baron's thoughts. "Not now that we've found his greyhound bitch."

This time von Studhoff allowed himself a smile. All men had their price, and this dog was Drummond's. By giving him what he desired, they could lure him into the trap.

"I went back to the couple who own her, as you said, and advised them to say nothing about that other problem."

The dog was apt to run out through any opened door, but the baron saw no reason for Drummond to know this. Not when things were falling so nicely in place.

Except for one detail. "Good, but we must deal with Lennox. I cannot like the frequency with which he visits."

"Never say you are jealous!"

The baron need only glare for the man's grin to fade. "As I suggested, you must prompt the chit to an indiscretion. Some embarrassment that shall induce Lennox to drop her. As a peer, he can ill afford to associate with a social pariah."

"Dip her in the scandal broth? But how?"

Spare me these unimaginative English dolts, the baron thought to himself. "Think," he resumed with forced patience. "What vice of hers can we best exploit?"

"Well, er, the gal's been known to gamble."

"There, then. Leave me, and go dream up some way to begin earning the massive sum I've been paying you."

All grumbling ceased, for the man knew who paid his considerable bills. Still, it was with more resentment than haste that he shuffled out of the tavern.

Watching him go, the baron felt quite pleased with himself. So much pleasure could be derived from manipulating others. And with a plump enough purse, he could bull his way through most any human obstacle.

He frowned, thinking of how much he depended on others to supply that purse. No matter. One day soon, if all went according to plan, he'd have no need for others to supply his funds; he would have fortune enough of his own.

And however unknowingly, Honor Drummond would lead him to it.

Geoff glared at the twisted knot. Instead of cascading in sartorial splendor, his cravat hung in a wrinkled mess.

With an oath, he tossed the linen on the floor atop the two other attempts and began work on another. This was why one hired a valet; he ought to find himself one soon.

Still, his fingers were accustomed to the task and the dratted cloth should have been tied long since, but he could concentrate on nothing with that incessant barking down in the stables—as well as the giggling down the hall.

He scowled. His cousins snickered over his earlier entry with Lolly. Excited by new surroundings, the dog had bounded through the narrow confines of his uncle's hallway with the same energy it must have displayed on the moors. Geoff caught up with the dog in the solarium, but it was not until he'd reached the parlor—where his aunt entertained Lady Jersey—that he could bring Lolly to an effective halt.

Unfortunately, this occurred perilously close to the tea tray, the contents of which liberally sprayed both his aunt and her guest. Their shrieks drew the entire household, the result of which had Lady Jersey stomping off in a huff, Aunt Maude taking to bed with the megrims, and Geoff being called again to his uncle's study.

With the dog still in tow, it had by needs been a short interview. His uncle shared the opinion that Miss Drummond's pet must find a new home at once, though for the time being, he allowed that the dog might reside in the stables.

Securing quarters for Lolly required a sizeable gratuity to his uncle's grooms, but considering the options—and all that barking—Geoff had happily paid the blunt.

Still, he must do something about getting rid of that dog. It was, he insisted as he marched from the room, the sole reason he was now going out to the Makepeace Ball.

From his study door, Lord Pithnevel watched his nephew leave the house. Dressed to the nines—save per-

haps for his cravat—he had plainly changed his mind
about staying home.

Smiling, Pithnevel rang for his butler. It was time to tell
the groom that the dog's barking was no longer required.

Geoff frowned as he entered the ballroom. With the Regent entertaining at Carlton House and the Melbournes
holding another soiree, Lady Makepeace's affair was not
quite the crush she had hoped it to be. Though in his opinion, there certainly seemed to be boors and prigs enough.

Like in his clubs, it was all so tediously predictable. All
the same faces, the same conversations. Although this late
in the Season, there was a certain desperation to the titters
behind the female fans, the remaining swains being either
the most difficult to snare, or the least desirable.

He saw several people he'd like to avoid, but nowhere
could he find Miss Drummond.

Every matron in the place seemed to locate *him*, going
on in length about her various unattached female relations
and his duty to the Lennox line. Indeed, such badgering
grew so intolerable, Geoff was prepared to snap at the next
unwary crone to tap his arm.

Where in blazes was Honor Drummond?

When the music started up, he took to the shadows, refusing to dance if he could in any way prevent it. As far
as he could see, there were about two sorts of females in
attendance: those with a predatory gleam, and those out
for fun. He had no intention to marry, and he was most
certainly in no mood for levity.

And upon that thought, he turned to find the Gratham
twins beaming up at him.

"Geoffrey," Amanda gushed, "we've found you at last!"

"Do let go of the poor man's sleeve." Pandora giggled.
"What good will all our hunting do, dearest M, if you now
frighten our quarry away?"

"But, P, I am ever so happy to see him again."

Abandoning their pet names, the twins had taken to using initials instead. They insisted they simply could not go about as Andy, Mandy, and Pandy, but bouncing about with them was such a happy part of his youth, and Geoff continued to think of all three Grathams as he'd always done. "Mandy," he said, kissing one hand—and "Pandy," kissing the other—barely resisting the urge to add, "Where is Andy?"

"Look at us," Pandy directed when the process was done. "Don't we look grand?"

They did indeed. Their golden ringlets were gathered in sophisticated knots atop their heads, while their high-waisted muslin gowns artfully emphasized their youthful figures. Knowing she'd an eye for such things, Geoff felt certain their older sister chose the outer trappings, but Andy, home preparing for her wedding, could exert no control over what went on in their pretty heads. Outwardly, the twins might be the very crack of fashion, but inside they were the same silly imps they had always been.

"You're in fine form," he offered, feeling a familiar wariness. "But what the deuce are you doing here in London?"

"Isn't it famous?" Pandy spoke, being the more lively of the pair. "Seems we are to have our Season after all."

"Indeed. Don't tell me you've decided to chase after dukes and now mean to toss over poor Adam and Jamie?"

"Not a bit of it." Pandy had that glint in her eye, the one that meant mischief. "Our weddings shall not be announced until after Andy has had hers. In truth, Geoff, the reason we've come to London is to find you a wife."

Unnerving, how her expression reminded him of Bellington. Shackled, they'd make a dangerous pair.

"Don't be a tease, P." The reprimand came from the more soft-spoken Amanda as she shot a warning glance her twin sister's way. "What P means to say, Geoff, is that Lady Sarah has decreed we need town bronzing."

Intercepting the look that passed between them, Geoff grew more uneasy. They were up to something and, given their past exploits, it could only spell disaster. The twins meant well, but their brains were like bubbles, designed more for froth and fun than intricate plotting.

"We feel dreadful over the way things came about for you and Andy," Pandy went on determinedly. "We truly thought we could bring you together, but . . . well . . . the least we can do now is find you another suitable female."

Amanda groaned—or perhaps he did—but Pandy was not to be halted. "Merely supply a name, dearest Geoff, and we shall see you matrimonialized before the Season is done."

He most definitely groaned at that.

"I'll wager my month's allowance we can lead you to the altar," Pandy boasted, wagging a finger at him.

Matchmaking on his behalf? Geoff saw he must put a stop to this at once. "Ladies do not gamble," he said sternly. "You should be ashamed of yourselves."

"Don't be such a stick. Betting is the absolute rage. Why, Jamie wagers all the time."

"All the more reason you should not, puss. The Bellington fortunes do have a bottom, you know."

"Pooh, Geoff. As if you yourself never indulge. Why, I've heard rumors—"

"I categorically refuse to take your allowance," he interrupted, not anxious to have the subject pursued.

Momentarily stumped, Pandy turned to her twin. Amanda shrugged and remarked that Geoff had always admired Papa's battle sword. "The sword it is then," Pandy announced, folding her arms with great satisfaction across her chest.

Geoff stifled a grin. "Have you stopped to think, you gooses, that Andy might not wish you to give it away?"

"Because it belonged to Papa? If she were that sentimental, why did she give you his snuffbox?"

"Oh, P, that was to keep Papa from pawning it," Amanda said quietly. "You know she hated how he sold everything for another round at the tables."

Geoff barely heard. He was thinking of Andy's lovely features as she'd presented the box. "So you might never forget me," she'd said so solemnly as she set it in his palm.

Nor had he. All these years, he'd meant to return for her, carelessly assuming she'd be content to wait. Taking the snuffbox from his vest pocket, he looked at it with regret. He'd miss the silly thing, but perhaps it was time to bid farewell to it—and that part of his life as well.

"Here," he said to the twins. "Take the thing."

Both gazed at him in bewilderment. "Papa's snuffbox?" Amanda asked, upon which Pandy explained that of course, Geoff meant to offer it as his part of the wager. How careless of them to forget to ask for his half, though heaven knew, the parson's mousetrap ought to be price enough.

It was indeed. Still, Geoff was not about to take on any more bets. He already risked his horses, his friendship with Foxley and Bellington, and his affection for Lady Sarah. "I have no intention of meeting your bet," he told them dryly. "Indeed, I think you ought to give up this particular vice. You're not very good at it."

"We shall see about that," Pandy said in a foreboding tone as she turned to flounce away.

Being with the twins must weaken the brain, Geoff decided as he watched them waltz off. How else could he have missed such a golden opportunity? If he must be trapped in yet another ridiculous wager, why hadn't he bet the dog?

Shaking his head, he made his way to the refreshment table, finding far more cloth than sustenance there. A sparse assortment of cake crumbs littered the occasional plate, and a sole ice, once rendered to resemble Wellington, had dwindled into a pitiful lump in the punch. Ladling himself a glass, Geoff held little hope that the liquid would prove worthy of its name.

He was frowning—for the drink was indeed insipid—when Lady Sarah joined him. "Amelia ever was a pinch-penny," she grumbled, likewise scowling at the bowl, "though since she's given up betting with me, one would think she could afford a creditable punch. Don't suppose there's an ounce of liquor in it?"

"I fear not."

"And she's the gall to wonder why half the ton is at Melbourne House." Lady Sarah reached for a cup. "She's over there, you know," she said without warning, clearly expecting Geoff to know which *she* Lady Sarah might mean.

The worst of it was, he did know, even before he followed the old woman's gaze. With a sense of relief he found all out of proportion, Geoff had found Honor Drummond at last.

∽ 8 ∽

General Drummond was not happy to be at the Makepeace Ball; the purchase of new, formal clothing seemed a useless expenditure of his dwindling cash. Still, Lady Sarah insisted it would help pave Honor's way back into Society's good graces, and in his heart, Drummond knew he owed it to his dear, beloved Evelyn to see their daughter settled well.

One could wish von Studhoff would stay beside them, but he seemed intent upon partnering every chit in the room. Poor Honor, Drummond thought, but when he looked at his daughter, he found it was not the baron at whom she gazed so wistfully, but Lennox instead.

Directed there by Lady Sarah, Geoff had been looking at Honor, unable to pull his gaze away. Again bedecked in muted colors, she was flanked on one side by her father, with von Studhoff standing sentinel on the other. In all that gray, she seemed rather like a partridge caught in a trap. Geoff found himself thinking she'd be a lovely thing, set free—that it would be exhilarating to watch her take flight.

But that thought smacked of the poetical, and Geoff was not—nor ever would be—the least bit romantic.

Impatient with such fancy, he might have turned away, had her lashes not then fluttered upward. As their gazes met, he found he was the one now snared.

And then, with a quirk of the lips, she winked at him!

He tried to be outraged, even disapproving, but a note of admiration slipped into his regard. She'd turned the tables on him so audaciously, he couldn't quite stop himself from grinning back.

Geoff felt the jab of Lady Sarah's cane. "Ask her to dance," she barked. "Show the young swains she don't bite."

Geoff could insist until dawn that he'd no wish to be punished by that dangerous walking stick, but in all honesty, the prospect of dancing no longer loomed so unpleasantly.

He made his way toward Miss Drummond. It was, after all, a mindless country dance, so there was no need to bother overmuch with conversation, and besides, he truly must settle the matter of her dog.

By the time he reached the Drummonds, the baron had decamped, but Geoff's relief withered under the general's less than enthusiastic regard. It was the man's eyes that spoke, not his lips, but the message was nonetheless clear. Geoff might now be the earl of Lennox, a veritable darling of the ton, but in the Drummond household he would always remain food for the general's dogs.

Gritting his teeth, Geoff politely inquired after their healths, their trip from Scotland, and the state of affairs at the War Office. He even asked after the baron, to which the general grumbled that the man had gone off to partner Miss Blackledge in the set being made up. In that case, Geoff suggested, he and Miss Drummond should then share a bounce across the floor. This did not make the general happy, but since his daughter had already placed her hand in Geoff's, there was little the man could politely do.

"I want to thank . . ." Miss Drummond began as they faced off for the set.

"I need to . . ." Geoff said at the same time, causing them both to smile. "Please," he added, "say your piece first."

But the music began, forcing them to go their separate ways. As she twirled off in one direction and he went through the steps in the other, Geoff watched her every move. Despite the drabness of her gown, she was in her best looks this evening. With her rosy cheeks and twinkling eyes, she possessed an undeniable zest, Geoff decided, an infectious exuberance not even von Studhoff could dampen entirely.

He became so fascinated by the pleasure she could derive from a simple country dance, when they came together, he quite forgot about the dog.

"Isn't this wonderful?" she gushed, slightly out of breath. "I just adore dancing. You can't imagine how I missed it in Scotland. Aunt Regina considers all form of revelry a crime. She forbade me to even hum a tune."

"Ah, you sing, then?"

"Can't hold a note," she admitted with an impish grin. "Which might be another reason my aunt forbade it."

He had time to chuckle before she spun off again, like a butterfly fluttering out of reach, and he was filled with the insane urge to go chasing after her.

He didn't, of course, but he did count the steps until the dance brought her back to him. Smiling down, anxious to resume their chatter, he might not have noticed that Richard Duncan had strolled into the room, had he not heard someone mention that Andy stood at his arm.

And in that moment, Geoff's entire world stopped.

* * *

Honor also looked up, wondering why Lennox paused. Her first thought was that she must have stepped on his foot, or said something wrong, but one glance at his face revealed that Honor Drummond was the farthest thing from his mind.

She looked over her shoulder, but she already knew who she would see there. One could not spend these last few weeks in London and not hear the talk about Geoff's regard for Miss Gratham.

With a sinking heart, Honor saw now how she'd been deluding herself. There was no use in learning how to charm him. One glimpse at such naked longing told her that she could flirt until her lashes drooped, but Lennox would never manage more than a minor affection for her.

He was in love with Andrea Gratham.

She tried to tell herself it hardly mattered, that she could easily find another earl to supplant the baron, but the hurt and disappointment built until they threatened to swamp her. The thing of it was, she had seen how lovely it could be. Nay, she had *felt* it. Here, on the dance floor as Lennox grinned down at her, she had known the fun and magic that two people of one mind could share.

Too late, she realized how much she actually *liked* the man. Oh, his lordship could grumble a good veneer, but down deep, however carefully he tried to conceal it, Lennox owned the oft-mentioned heart of gold. Lucky Lolly could find no finer—albeit temporary—home.

If only she could have found one there as well.

Aware that the dance had gone on around them, that other couples now stared in curious fashion, Honor knew she must not stay where she was so plainly ignored and unwanted. Biting her lip, she muttered a quick, unconvincing excuse and promptly took her leave.

She doubted Lennox even heard her.

* * *

He hadn't; he only knew that she was gone. Facing the scowls and titters, he discovered he now had to explain to the others why they had failed to finish the set.

Confounded chit, he thought as he made inane apologies and left the dance floor. They had been having a perfectly splendid time when . . .

Uneasily, he remembered how he had halted at the sight of Andy's lovely face. How soft and feminine she'd seemed in her fashionable gown, yet so unattainable. Gazing at her, Geoff had seen all that he might have had, but lost.

Richard was the wisest of chaps to stand guard beside her. A bit more vigilance on Geoff's part and he could have been standing there in his stead.

But the more Geoff gazed at them, the more he saw how Richard and Andy fit together like the pieces of a puzzle, how they complemented each other in the glances they exchanged. Theirs was a secret understanding, and it went beyond any affection Andy and Geoff might ever have shared.

And strangely enough, it was at that exact moment he'd remembered his dancing partner.

Miss Drummond had not twirled on with the music, he'd discovered, but rather remained at his side, her wide eyes regarding him with a sea of concern, and perhaps a certain bewilderment. He should have said something, he saw now, for before he could blink, she'd flitted off to resume her dutiful post beside the baron.

"I see London is treating you well," Richard said suddenly at his side. "Though I can't say the same for your valet. You might better have tied that cravat yourself."

Andy, standing beside him, chuckled softly. "I daresay he did. Knowing Geoff, he has not yet employed a manservant. He never did like having others fuss over him."

Perhaps Andy had been right, Geoff decided irritably, in

claiming they knew each other far too well to risk marriage. She would never dare tease Richard so. "So, what are you two doing in town?" he asked to change the subject.

Andy grinned. "I'm to be bronzed. Lady Sarah seems to think I need some town polish. Can you imagine? She actually expects me to learn how to dance."

Aware of her inadequacies on that score, Geoff laughed.

"Just so." She gave him a rueful grin. "But still, we mean to humor the dear, at least until another diversion can absorb her time. Given her addiction to matchmaking, we'd hoped to settle her interests in that direction. I say, you don't know of a likely victim, do you, Geoff? What of the young lady with whom you were just dancing?"

"Honor Drummond?" he asked with a guilty start, aware that he still watched her intently. "Hate to disappoint you, Andy gal, but I fear she's already taken. By the baron von Studhoff." He nodded at the unlikely pair.

"Such a taking thing, married to that old prig," Andy gasped. "Oh, Geoff, you must be mistaken."

"She's not exactly married yet," he felt moved to add. "Not until the end of the month."

Richard grinned, his gaze following Geoff's across the room. "I remember Honor. Never guess it to look at her now, but she once had a delightful sense of humor. Had an unusual way of looking at things too, as I recall."

"She sounds just the sort of female I'd most like to meet." Andy levelled her most considering gaze on Geoff. "Do be a dear and introduce us."

Disconcerted, Geoff did his utmost to protest, but Andy had always bullied him. It was the very reason she'd given for refusing his offer, he recalled. She'd said Geoff was too nice to ever tell her no.

She must have been right, for in the end, he made the introduction. The baron, effusive about meeting the earl of

Fairbright, did his best to monopolize the conversation. Not that this fazed Drummond, who barely acknowledged anyone, while his daughter, showing none of her earlier spark, answered Andy's proddings in mere monosyllables.

Irrationally enough, Geoff felt disappointed. He found he'd wanted them to like Miss Drummond, but he could see no hope for this as long as she persisted in playing the mouse.

And as if this were not irksome enough, Fortesque must wander over to complete their less than lively set. Geoff feared the man meant to badger him about their wager, but it was Miss Drummond he'd come to pester instead. "Made any good bets lately?" he asked her softly.

She blushed, sent an anxious glance at the baron, and replied just as quietly that she'd given up the vice.

With a shake of his head, Fortesque turned to Geoff. "Hope you haven't taken it into your head to reform, too, old chap. Heard Mortimer and Spencer plan to race tomorrow. Hard to resist such odds, eh?"

The difficulty, Geoff well knew, would be in finding anyone foolish enough to back Mortimer, the worst whip in London. He said as much to Fortesque.

"Foolish? Afraid to back a long shot, Stone?"

"I believe the correct address is Lennox." Two spots of color appeared in Miss Drummond's cheeks, as if she too were annoyed by the man. "The *earl* of Lennox."

Geoff, trying not to smile, told himself that he could fight his own battles, thank you all the same.

"But what of you, Honor, my dear?" Fortesque persisted. "Not like *you* to shy away from a long shot. How well I recall the many times you proved the oddsmakers wrong."

A reluctant grin came to her lips, but she checked the impulse with a swift glance to the baron. "I have no further interest in such pursuits," she said woodenly. "I prefer to forget that part of my imprudent youth."

Fortesque went on, insisting he knew better, and would no doubt have continued badgering had Andy not interrupted with a question of her own. As Miss Drummond turned to answer her, Fortesque jabbed Geoff in the ribs. "See? I told you, quite reformed," the fool taunted in a snide whisper. "You haven't a prayer of keeping your horses."

Geoff thought the man must be blind. Even in his own short acquaintance with Miss Drummond, Geoff knew the key barometer to her reactions lay in those expressive eyes. Any fool could see her discomfort in the nervous glances to the baron, but Geoff alone seemed to notice her longing. She ached to watch the race tomorrow. And given but the slightest opportunity, she would happily make that bet.

He very nearly found himself offering to escort her, but was spared such folly by the arrival of Hermione and Iris. Looking smug, they perched on either side of Miss Drummond like the guardian angels they proclaimed themselves to be. Fortesque made a hasty excuse and took himself off, with Richard and Andy swiftly following suit. It was no doubt his cousins who also prompted the baron to announce that it was late and that he and the Drummonds too must be off.

Watching Honor trail off behind von Studhoff, Geoff found no reason to linger. Odd, but he felt dazed, as if swept up by a whirlwind, and then set back down, with his own safe emotions replaced with a fresh set of unfamiliar ones.

All the way home, he kept thinking he'd forgotten something, left some item undone, but it was not until he drove into the stables and heard the welcoming yap that he recalled why he'd gone to the ball. That confounded dog!

He muttered an oath. Very well, he must simply drive back to the Drummonds, and make Miss Drummond deal with her own pet.

But as Lolly jumped up beside him, lavishly exuberant in its greeting, Geoff conceded that perhaps the silly animal could be allowed to stay the night.

But tomorrow, after he'd watched the race . . .

In his mind, he could see that telltale gleam in Miss Drummond's eyes, and he realized there was no real need to stir himself to action at this late hour. He could as easily wait for the morning.

After all, he knew precisely where he would find her.

~9~

Miss Drummond did not disappoint him.

It was not Geoff who found her the following morning, however; Lolly, perched on the seat beside him, gave the identifying bark as it jumped down to greet its mistress.

Off from the crowd and tucked amidst the trees, Miss Drummond had brought along her maid and a footman, an attempt at propriety undermined by guilty glances over her shoulder. Geoff, who suspected her vehicle might have again been purloined from her father, tried hard to remain unamused, but the joy with which dog and mistress greeted each other could bring a smile to a stone.

Yet even as the grin began to form, Fortesque came up from the right.

Geoff could not like this. The man had a bloodhound's skill at scenting out the latest *on dit*. Alighting, Geoff tied his team to a tree and went to offer whatever protection Miss Drummond might require.

"What I meant," Fortesque was explaining as he oh-so-casually led Miss Drummond away from her servants, "is I myself can hardly resist the odds. Why, I stand to triple my investment should he win. Been practicing daily,

Mortimer has, ever since his aunt died and left him those chestnuts. Never saw a finer pair, I can tell you, unless one considers Lennox' cattle. Still, he ain't racing Lennox, is he? No, indeed, it's Spencer he's up against, and between you and me, I think we can make a sizeable killing from this day's work."

"A 'killing'?"

"A profit, dear girl. And a tidy one, at that. See, I've brought the betting book with me. All you need do is sign your name, right here...."

Too well, Geoff could picture him holding court at White's, pointing to her name and using it to draw the curious around him. Seeing Miss Drummond take the book, he quickened his pace.

"I am sorry, but I have so little to wager," he heard her say, her brows furrowing as she studied the names. Geoff wondered if she'd recognize that they were all male.

"The amount is unimportant. The bet's the thing."

There had been rumors that Fortesque had become a Captain Sharp, that he now supported his considerable habit by luring young gapeseeds into the less-than-respectable dens of London, but only an utter cad would stoop to gulling poor, trusting females. Geoff flexed his fingers, for they itched to land a facer square in the man's jaw.

With that extra sense animals seem to possess, Lolly began his infamous yapping. He came bounding back to Geoff, jumping up and pulling at his hand as if hoping to lead both man and fist to Fortesque's chin.

"Ah, here you are, Miss Drummond." Geoff improvised, now that their attention was focused on himself. "Lady Sarah sent me to offer apologies. I fear she has had to leave. Seems to be suffering from some stomach disorder."

"Lady Sarah?" Fortesque, normally pasty-faced enough, now blanched to match his linen.

There had been tales, Geoff recalled, of that lady using her infamous cane on Fortesque, after he'd swindled her grandson. "To be precise, she *was* here," he said, watching Miss Drummond stifle a grin. "Before she left, however, she requested I escort her goddaughter home. 'To rescue the gal from undesirable elements' is how she phrased it."

Fortesque now viewed Miss Drummond with considerable alarm. Grabbing the book, he hid it behind him. "Heavens, look at the time. I should return to . . . to my party. To watch the race." Spinning on a heel, he transferred the bundle to his front as he rapidly took his leave.

"Sorry to interrupt," Geoff said as he watched Fortesque scurry off, betting book clutched to his chest, "but that man's an out-and-out bounder. He's been known to lead many a lad to ruin with his 'certain' schemes."

"But I wasn't—"

"I should warn that he has rather loose lips, as well. Most of the *on dits* about town seem to come out of them."

"But I—"

"And while I can understand an occasional desire to gamble, Miss Drummond, might I point out that you would be wiser to employ more private channels?"

She tilted her head.

"A betting book is so public," he felt compelled to explain. "Your name would be bandied about in every club in London." When she still did not speak, or look one whit chastened, he added with exasperation, "If you must place wagers, could you not find a more reliable gentleman?"

"A reliable gentleman?" Her lips quirked. "Are you perchance suggesting yourself, my lord?"

"At least I . . ." he started, getting very much upon his dignity, until he noticed the glint in her eyes. *Why, she's teasing*, he thought. "I'll have you know," he told her with a grin, "I'm quite the expert in all matters of speculation."

"So I have heard." She began to laugh, a contagious sound. "Oh, dear me. I had quite made up my mind not to wager at all, you should know, but while I found it fairly simple to remain immune to Fortesque's taunts, I now fear that between your reliability *and* your expertise, you might have placed too great a temptation before me."

Geoff was surprised by how much he enjoyed their banter. Studying her, he found the royal blue carriage dress and matching bonnet did much for her looks. He could wish, though, that more of her golden locks might escape, that perhaps he, and not the breeze, could play with the strands about her face.

"I suppose I must choose Mortimer," she said. "Not only are the odds irresistible, but his new pair is rumored to rival your own."

"Never!"

She tilted her head again to stare at him. "If you prefer to withdraw your offer . . ."

"I *never* back down from a wager. What are the stakes to be?"

She grinned. "Nothing as mundane as money, I hope. I do not have an abundant supply of it."

None of the wagers Geoff made lately were worthwhile; why should this be any different? "I daresay we could bet the dog." He gestured at Lolly, panting at her side.

"Oh my." Coloring, she looked down at the animal. "I never did properly thank you for saving Lolly's life. What an utter ingrate you must think me."

"Please." Geoff, oddly embarrassed, held up a hand to stop her. "I did no more than anyone else might have done."

She shook her head. "Do not go overmodest on me. Should the general realize Lolly is alive, he will happily murder him." She looked up, eyes so impossibly green Geoff feared he might become lost in them. "I meant to thank you properly last night, but the mere mention of Lolly's name can send the general into apoplexy."

Geoff now remembered her trying to speak before the dance split them apart. And how, after that, the general had always been within earshot.

"I had no intention of so abusing your generosity," she went on. "I'd have come for Lolly yesterday, the instant the baron gave me a moment alone, but it was so late when he left."

Geoff, gazing into her eyes, decided only a proper blackguard could give her dog over to Drummond's rage.

But before he could find a solution, a small boy, legs pumping at twice the speed of his upper torso, rounded the curve in the road. "Here they come!" he shouted, even as the slow, building thunder of hoofbeats shook the ground.

"Oh my!" Miss Drummond gasped, even as she hurried back to her carriage. "The race! It has begun!"

Fortesque barely heard the race, being too preoccupied with worry. The baron would not be pleased with this at all. Drat, but must Stone ruin everything he hoped to do?

He refused to call the man Lennox. In Fortesque's mind, it was sheer injustice that a profligate like Stone should be granted a title and fortune, while he himself had to grovel to men like the baron.

And von Studhoff would not be pleased to learn that Stone had come to Miss Drummond's rescue this morning.

Just why had he? Fortesque wondered. Rogues weren't likely to so bestir themselves, not to keep a reckless chit's name from being bandied about in the clubs. More likely, Stone meant to use his looks and charm to turn her head, knowing a girl as green as Honor Drummond was apt to take such flattery seriously. Why, she might even grow bold enough to reject the baron.

Fortesque frowned. If she did, he stood to lose not only that wager, but his income from the baron, as well.

Double drat that Stone, what was a man to do?

As if in answer, someone shouted out that the racers had come in neck to neck, and that the contest must be repeated. His spirits lightened at once, for as surely as the sun would rise, Miss Drummond would return for the second competition.

And tomorrow, he swore to himself, he would find some way to get her alone.

~10~

Miss Drummond stared wistfully after Mortimer and Spencer as they continued down the road at decreasing speeds. "Oh, I had forgotten how much fun this can be."

Geoff smiled in complete empathy. "No better way to spend a morning. A good thing they mean to run this race again. A tie could have proved a messy affair."

She looked at him, tilting her head. "Messy?"

"Splitting your dog in half. We both won, after all."

Her eyes began to twinkle. "Ah, but we both lost, as well. Besides, if the race is to be repeated, I shall have a second chance to win that wager."

"Second chance, indeed. Do you intend to sneak out of the house again?"

To his surprise, she made no attempt to deny she had done so, smiling sheepishly instead. "It is not at all the thing, is it? But I ask you, my lord, what would you do in my place? Sit contentedly in some stuffy parlor waiting to hear the results, or watch the race yourself?"

"I quite see your point. But then, I am not the one you must convince, Miss Drummond. Dare I suggest it is time I returned you to your father?"

"Do not trouble yourself, my lord. I have Betsy here, and—"

"Have you forgotten Fortesque?" Gesturing to where the man still eyed them from afar, Geoff pressed his point. "If I fail to escort you home now, he might question that drivel about Lady Sarah's illness. The man's an incurable gossip. Both your father and the baron might yet learn of your being here this morning."

Her face fell. Indeed, it was suddenly so devoid of animation, Geoff wished he had never mentioned the German lout at all. "You," he called over his shoulder to her servants as he ushered Miss Drummond toward his curricle. "Follow us home, if you please. Your mistress shall ride with me."

Hearing the word *ride*, Lolly gave a short yap and bounded up into the curricle. "I doubt we could find a better chaperon," Geoff grumbled good-naturedly. "Can't budge the beast from that seat when it thinks I need company."

"*It*, my lord?" Miss Drummond let the tiniest grin play across her face as he helped her into the carriage. "Hasn't Lolly yet convinced you that he's at least half human?"

Smiling reluctantly, Geoff joined both woman and dog on the seat. "Now that you point it out, I do see something in the dog that bears a certain resemblance to Lady Sarah. I don't suppose it owns a cane?"

With a laugh, she hugged the dog affectionately, only to draw back. "Oh my," she gasped, wrinkling her pretty nose. "He's quite ripe, isn't he?"

"Lolly's been staying in the stables," Geoff explained defensively. "It was the best I could manage."

"Oh, but I'm certain he's had a perfect lark. Lolly adores horses. Indeed, I've often wondered if that is why he dislikes the baron so intensely. I'm told the man whips his mounts into submission."

She shivered and Geoff himself felt chilled as he wondered upon whom else the baron might feel justified in using his lash.

"Sorry, boy," Miss Drummond said to the dog, "but it'll be back to the kitchen for you now. The kitchen, and an immediate bath."

Geoff well remembered her last attempt in that quarter. "He might better stay in my uncle's stable a bit longer," he offered rashly, too preoccupied with steering the curricle toward town to properly consider the suggestion.

"I couldn't impose so." The protest was followed by a sheepish grin. "The truth is, I've missed Lolly dreadfully. I don't know how I shall ever manage when I must take him to his new home."

Geoff might have suspected female theatrics lay behind such a speech, but since Miss Drummond again hugged the dog without sparing her nose in the least, he was inclined to consider the emotion genuine. "Perhaps you might feel better if you were to know Lolly was settled in a suitable location. I can inquire about town. Among my acquaintances, there must be someone who wants a dog."

"You would go to such trouble? For me . . . I mean, for Lolly?"

He took his eyes from the road to glance at her. *But I adore rescuing damsels in distress,* he nearly blurted, until the curricle hit a rut and snapped him out of such idiocy. He'd said much the same on their first encounter, he recalled. It was not for him to remind her of the incident— not if she hadn't the decency to remember it herself.

"The thing of it is," she added quietly, "mine might not be a name you'd wish to mention to your friends."

He turned to look at her again.

"I am not quite the thing in Polite Society," she went on, staring at the gloved hands in her lap. "I know I've made many dreadful mistakes."

"I believe I was out of town at the time," Geoff said, hoping if she spoke about her past, she might remember his part in it. "Did these 'mistakes' involve murder, mayhem, or merely dueling at dawn?"

She smiled ruefully. "I never set out to be wicked. I just seem to have this deplorable talent for acting first and thinking too late. My drillmaster was forever chiding me about it."

"Your drillmaster?"

"I had a somewhat unusual education." She sighed. "The general was born and bred to the military life, you must understand. Being far too busy to raise a daughter, he turned to his staff, relegating the task to whoever might be on leave at the moment, or in need of extra cash. While other young ladies learned to embroider and hold polite conversation, I was taught to ride and shoot."

The words were flippant, but Geoff could hear the hurt behind them. No mother and no real father—what a lonely childhood she must have had.

"As a result, I never quite grasped what it was Society expected of me," she continued. "I came to London hoping to live life, to experience all it had to offer. By the time I understood the restrictions, that the rules for women differ drastically from those for men, I'd already made quite a muddle of things."

"Hence, the purloined phaeton."

She grinned reluctantly. "I will have you know, my lord, that a good many of the stunts with which I am credited are sheer fabrication."

"I am devastated to hear this." He shook his head in mock disappointment. "Does this mean that you never did kill a man in a duel?"

"Stewart was a good hundred yards away when we exchanged shots, and despite my tutors' unending patience, I cannot hit the Tower of London at twenty paces."

Geoff struggled not to smile. He should not let himself be amused, but sometimes, she made it deuced difficult to remember why not.

"I wish I could likewise deny the gambling," she went on, "but for years I'd been watching my tutors bet on anything, from the weather to the general's current disposition. They always made much of the victor and I thought, well, if I could just win a few wagers, perhaps people would stand up and take notice."

She didn't mention the hurt she must have felt, or the loneliness, but Geoff nonetheless knew it had been there.

"I began with Freddie Throckmorton," she said, "setting the hour upon which Countess Beason would fall asleep. I chose Freddie, since he never refused a wager, and the hour of eleven as I'd been watching the countess nod off for weeks."

"Hardly a challenge there."

"Quite so. But then, I *had* to win, for Freddie was bound to talk about my success. I next chose Fortesque, knowing he was no less addicted to gambling. We bet on the nature of Lady Violet's most current ailment." She said it so matter-of-factly, it was hard to remember that she was not a gentleman, mapping out his next move. "Of course, I had unfair prior knowledge, via my godmother, but Fortesque was quite sporting about the loss. He suggested another wager to recoup his losses, and before I knew it, I was betting all the time."

Geoff chuckled, not knowing if his reaction stemmed from the plan itself, or the fact that her victim was Fortesque. "I see. And thus began your life of crime?"

"More or less. I thrived on the attention, you see. Men would flock about me, not to flirt or ask me to dance, but rather to match my current wager. Each night I grew more inventive, more daring, though I never felt the need to drink like the men did. Indeed, I was so inebriated with the utter fun of it all, it was as if I were foxed all the time. I must confess, it was a jolly good time while it lasted."

Here it is, he thought. "And how did it stop?"

"The baron." As this was uttered with none of her prior enthusiasm, Geoff turned to study her face. She pointed forward, and following the gesture, Geoff saw a gaudy barouche turn into the square on their right. Cavendish Square, he realized with a jolt. Had she truly kept him so entertained, he'd failed to notice they had reached her home?

Reacting to her change in mood, Geoff pulled his team to the curb, letting the baron make the turn without them. Painted black, with garish gold trim and lettering, the barouche seemed a harbinger of doom. Miss Drummond, who had been so lively, looked as if she had just seen a ghost.

"I can't imagine what I was thinking of," she said quickly. "I cannot possibly go to that race tomorrow."

"I thought you wanted to live, to experience all life has to offer?" he said, unreasonably annoyed. "How can you be content to wait in some stuffy parlor for the results?"

She looked up in surprise, her eyes searching his.

"Drat, what a man doesn't know cannot hurt him. How can the baron be displeased if he never learns of the excursion?"

The impish grin returned. "My lord, you are not suggesting I again sneak out of the house?"

So he was, Geoff realized, matching her grin for grin. "I am told the man's toilette is so intricate, his valet can't complete it before noon. We shall be safe enough if we are gone by nine."

"Amazing." She did not wait for aid as she stepped down. "And here I thought you to be such a stick."

"We are all what we need to be," he said as he too alit.

"What's it to be, Miss Drummond? The parlour or my curricle?"

"I suppose I must accompany you. Knowing how you covet my dog, I cannot take the chance that you might cheat."

"Never call a man a cheat, else he might be induced to call you out. Despite your inability to hit the Tower of London."

It was such utter pleasure, watching her laugh, until he grew aware of heads turning their way. This would not do at all; the woman could ill afford the attention.

"I cannot leave you here at the curb," he told her, instantly sobering. "I'd as soon risk the baron's wrath by escorting you to your door."

She shook her head. "That is kind of you, my lord, but there is a back entrance. I think it wiser that I sneak into the house that way. As you said—what the man doesn't know can never hurt him."

"And your servants? Can you fit that carriage in the back door?"

She looked at her maid and footman, discreetly waiting on the curb behind them. "I can go with them. Please, it is best if the baron does not see you. For everyone."

She reached down for Lolly, and for some bizarre reason, Geoff reached out to stop her. "You can never convince me that you can sneak this oaf of a dog past the baron."

She frowned. "Dear me. I had quite forgotten why he's come so early this morning. He must have found that new greyhound he means to give the general to start his kennel."

"Then all things considered, perhaps Lolly had best stay with me."

"But his bath . . ."

"I can see to the mongrel's grooming. I shall make certain he'll be a proper dandy for our excursion tomorrow."

She looked up at him, her gaze once again measuring. "No, most definitely not a stick. I daresay you are the nicest gentleman I know."

She turned, taking her charming smile with her, leaving Geoff to grab the dog before it could follow. By the time he resettled Lolly on the seat, Miss Drummond and her servants were turning the corner.

Realizing that he was staring quite stupidly after her, Geoff shook himself and started home. He drove to his uncle's house in the same daze he always seemed to feel when he quit her presence, although some knowledge of his folly was already sifting down to his common sense.

What could he have been thinking of, offering to spirit her off from her father's house in the dead of morning? This was just the sort of prank he and Andy might have dreamed up in their youth, but he was an adult now, a peer of the realm, and should he continue in this vein, he would soon prove himself the very cad the general had branded him.

Nor was his conscience assuaged when he reached the stables to find Pithnevel awaiting him there.

"If I could but have a moment of your time?" his uncle asked before Geoff could hop down from the curricle.

Geoff cringed inwardly, for he could guess Pithnevel's reaction upon learning he'd led Miss Drummond into the very scandal he'd been asked to prevent. "I am quite busy at the moment. Lolly needs a bath."

Pithnevel wrinkled his nose. "Indeed. But we have servants to do that."

Geoff shrugged as he went about unhitching his team. Both tasks could as easily be done by the grooms, but Geoff derived a certain satisfaction in caring for his own.

"So how goes it with Miss Drummond?" Pithnevel

asked. "I assume she is not yet ready to resume care of her dog?"

"I daresay it will be some time before she can do so, since the baron seems to be presenting the general with a new greyhound. Miss Drummond doesn't wish to risk tainting yet another of her father's prized litters."

"A greyhound? As a gift?"

"So she said. Say," Geoff added, turning suddenly to ask, "I don't suppose you know of anyone who needs a dog? Preferably someone with a home in the country?"

"What? Er, no." As if embarrassed to be caught wool-gathering, Pithnevel pulled himself to attention. "We have a difficult situation here. Von Studhoff has raised objections about the attention you've been paying Honoria. Drummond now feels you might be a bad influence on his girl."

"Of all the—"

"I've explained to Drummond that you are quite harmless, but both he and the baron are adamant. As Miss Drummond will be staying here while the general goes out of town, he has requested you find other living quarters."

Harmless? Geoff thought with resentment. It didn't help to realize that the suggestion was the decent thing to do. He should have thought to make the arrangements himself, but once again, he was found wanting in his uncle's eyes.

"However," Pithnevel went on, surprising him yet again, "I would rather keep you near at hand. As such, I have taken the liberty of turning out the gentleman's apartment at the top of the stables. It has not been used since your uncle Jack passed on, and as I recall . . . well, you might in the end choose to stay at your club. I do hope you will consider remaining, though. As a favor to me."

Geoff could only stare. Pithnevel *wanted* him to stay? And he had asked, not ordered him to do so?

"Good," his uncle said, taking Geoff's assent for

granted as he turned to go. How like him to make his exit the instant he had what he wanted.

"Oh, one thing more," he added from the door. "About this greyhound. You're quite certain von Studhoff presented it as a gift?"

"So Miss Drummond said."

"Hmmm," Pithnevel said as he walked off.

Perplexed, Geoff stared after him. Odd, the way his uncle harped upon that greyhound.

Lolly barked suddenly, as if Geoff had spoken aloud. "There will be no greyhounds for you," he told the dog with a laugh. "For you, there will be a bath."

Lolly got that look in his eyes, well-remembered from their first meeting.

A bath, indeed!

~11~

Von Studhoff sat at his club, his gaze on his glass of port, but his mind miles away. Drummond's butler might think he'd been fobbed off with that nonsense about Miss Drummond having a headache, but the baron had seen her in the curricle with Lennox.

He could not like the earl's sudden interest, or the silly chit's reaction to it. And considering the current developments in France, von Studhoff could ill afford to have Lennox get in his way.

Something must be done at once.

Uncomfortably aware that they were fast approaching the fashionable hour, Geoff forced himself to stroll through Hyde Park, scanning the bushes without an outward sign of panic.

Confound that Lolly! Didn't the mongrel realize half of London would soon be gathered along these paths, that a wet and soapy dog was bound to draw notice? Geoff must find Lolly and drag it home before they could be recognized. Once home, however, he'd gladly pay whatever necessary to his uncle's servants to have them complete the animal's bath.

"I say, Geoff. Where the deuce are you going in such a hurry? And without your curricle and pair."

If Jamie were in the park, the rest of the ton could not be far behind. There was no help for it; Geoff knew he must enlist his friend to aid in his search.

Yet before he could mouth the request, Adam hailed them. Having spent the past hour in Amanda Gratham's company, Adam could hear and talk of nothing else. Indeed, he proved so adamant in steering the conversation back to his beloved, Geoff found no way to wedge his own request into it.

"P wants to watch the race tomorrow," Jamie managed to get in, but only because he referred to Amanda's twin. "Suggested we make a party of it. You and M, Richard and Andy, and perhaps Geoff and ... I say, old boy, do you suppose you can find a female who could be coerced to go along?"

Geoff, who'd been scanning the scenery, turned back to his friends with a start. "Miss Drummond—" he began, meaning to tell them of his prior plans, but Jamie pounced.

"Geoff? And Honor Drummond?" he asked, overloud in his amazement. "By gads, P was right then. Tried to convince me there was something brewing here."

Secretly vowing that he must have a talk with that silly twin, Geoff did his best to mend the damage Pandy had done. "I am merely escorting Miss Drummond as a favor to Lady Sarah. Nothing more."

"Precisely what I told P." Jamie shook his head. "But you know females—so set on the romantical. She seems to think you're no longer immune to love."

"Love?" With a snort, Adam gave that statement the scorn it deserved. "As if Geoff paid the least attention to romance. Not that it would do him any good anyway. Everyone knows the general has taken him in dislike."

"I'd think the general should consider him the perfect escort," Jamie protested. "Peer of the realm, and all that."

Geoff, having no wish to reveal the true cause for the man's antipathy, barked out the more obvious explanation. "One can only assume he feels his daughter already has the perfect escort. Or had you forgotten Miss Drummond is engaged to the baron?"

"I suppose I had forgotten." Jamie grinned broadly. "But it certainly seems *you* have not."

"We could have the twins ask Lady Sarah," Adam suggested, ever ready to unruffle feathers. "I daresay she knows best how to deal with the general."

Geoff had to concede it was an ideal solution. He could not ignore the merits in gaining the general's permission beforehand—especially were it obtained by someone else.

Yet why, he wondered uneasily, did he feel such a twinge of disappointment at the fact that he and Miss Drummond would not spend the morning alone?

"I say, Geoff," Jamie said suddenly, looking over his shoulder behind them. "Isn't that your dog, chasing that greyhound?"

Following his outstretched hand, Geoff found that it was indeed Lolly. That the greyhound was a female—and a female in season—was evidenced by the tenacity of Lolly's pursuit.

No, Geoff thought. It cannot be; surely it was too much a coincidence that the baron had just presented Drummond with a new bitch for his kennels.

Bidding his friends an abrupt farewell, he raced after the dogs.

Both animals had ducked into the shrubbery before he could reach them. He looked all over for the frolicking pair, but when Lolly emerged from the bushes with what could only be termed a smirk, Geoff could see it was far too late.

As he groaned, he heard someone call out behind him, "Aphrodite?"

The greyhound stepped out of the bushes, its manner so disdainful even Lolly's irrepressible tail had to droop.

"Lolly," the voice whispered and Geoff turned to find Miss Drummond much as he'd last seen her, but *sans* bonnet and with hair a trifle more dishevelled. "Oh no, not again."

Geoff nodded. Biting a knuckle, she looked away. At first, he thought she meant to stifle a giggle—there was a certain black humor to the situation—but he could hear a telltale quiver in her voice. "I needed fresh air—the baron can be most stuffy when he lectures—and I only kept the door open for the slimmest of moments—but it is apparently all that Aphrodite needs."

"She escaped?"

She nodded, lowering her hands and grasping them before her. "I did not dare chase after her until I could convince the baron to leave. He shall be more than livid when he learns of . . . of this."

"Come, accidents happen. Even von Studhoff should be able to understand." Yet even as he said it, Geoff knew it was sheer drivel; the baron hadn't an understanding bone in his body. "And if he should not, perhaps we can convince him I am to blame."

She shook her head. "It will never do; he is angry enough with you as it is. Someone apparently saw us this morning and ran to him with the news. That was part of the reason he came to visit. To chastise me."

Geoff, annoyed that the baron seemed to have eyes and ears everywhere, spoke more sharply than he intended. "Very well, but I still see no need to volunteer information. We cannot know Aphrodite will have a litter. If and when it should arrive, you can merely act as baffled as everyone else. After all, your father thinks Lolly dead, doesn't he?"

"The general is dense, my lord, but not altogether witless. Even he is bound to see Lolly in those pups. He might even recognize him sooner, the way Lolly accompanies you everywhere."

"Yes, well, I've a reason for that. Been out trying to find the dog a proper home," he improvised. "In fact, I hope to have the matter settled before the week is out."

A blatant untruth, of course, but he'd be hanged by the toenails before he'd admit—even to himself—that he might enjoy having Lolly ride beside him.

"A home?" Miss Drummond asked, her voice going small. "Why, that's wonderful news."

Clearly, it was anything but, for a telltale moisture gathered in her eyes. Add another qualification to the dog's new home. Not only must the estate be large enough to accommodate an animal of its nature, but it must now be accessible to Miss Drummond's visits as well.

In his mind, he could picture Lolly sprinting across the verdant hills of the Lennox estate, himself and Miss Drummond following at a slower, more enjoyable pace. Kent was not so very far from Drummond House, he thought pleasurably, that she might not stop by now and then.

"Geoff! I must say, the way you bounded off, we feared—oh, Miss Drummond—"

Jamie stopped in his tracks, glancing from said lady to Geoff, while Adam divided his gaze between the dogs. Both gentlemen grinned broadly.

As Geoff tried to formulate an explanation, a sporty new curricle tooled by on the path to their right. The fop holding the ribbons proved far too besotted to see more than the Fashionable Impure at his side, but Geoff knew it was but the first of many carriages that would soon pass their way. "Miss Drummond was just going home," he spoke out, conscious of the need to remove her from the public eye.

She stared at him, then at Adam and Jamie. "Of course," she said at last, both tone and manner subdued as she reached for the greyhound's collar. "I had not meant to embarr—er, detain you."

"I say, Miss Drummond," Jamie blurted, "would you mind if we accompanied you home? Might as well speak to your father now. About your joining us at the race to-morrow."

Her eyes went straight to Geoff.

"Geoff didn't mention it?" Adam followed her gaze speculatively. "How remiss of him. We're making up a party. The Gratham twins, their sister Andrea—"

"Andrea Gratham?" Like the glance, her question was aimed not at Jamie, but rather at Geoff. "I see." Dropping her gaze, she tugged ruthlessly at the greyhound's collar. "Come along then. I daresay this is as good a time as any to speak to the general. Perhaps you can keep him occupied so I can sneak Aphrodite back into the house."

She started off, not bothering to bid Geoff farewell, nor even looking back at him. Stung, he might yet have included himself in their party, had Lolly not tried to do the same. Foreseeing problems, for Aphrodite snarled at him, Geoff grabbed the mutt by its collar.

"Women!" he said under his breath, and Lolly whimpered in canine agreement. "Tomorrow can only be a disaster."

∞ 12 ∞

This is bound to be a disaster, Honor was thinking as she watched the first vehicle arrive in the square. It was bad enough that Lennox felt a need to overinflate the party, but must he add to the slight by filling his curricle with those cousins of his?

And fill it they did, she thought spitefully, for Iris and Hermione seemed overly snug on that seat. It would serve him right if they chattered and nagged the entire way.

Behind Lennox, in a curricle of his own, drove the obnoxious Horatio Duncan. *His* vehicle was empty, she noticed with chagrin; clearly, she was expected to ride with him.

Still, any outing was better than none, and wanting to be off before the general—who was yet reading his paper—could change his mind, she snatched her bonnet and raced out the door before Lennox could reach the bell.

He seemed startled to see her, for he pulled up short, and for an instant, she thought she saw a marked appreciation for her bottle green carriage gown, and the extra care she'd taken in her toilette. Honor would happily have spent hours just staring into his soft gray eyes, but

Hermione said something she could not hear, after which the most fearsome scowl came to Lennox' face.

With a great clatter, the ponderous Fairbright coach rounded the corner and Lennox turned his attention to it. On her part, Honor looked to the open carriage with the hope that there might be a spot for her, but between Lady Sarah, the Gratham twins, Richard and Andrea, her only chance of eluding Horatio's company would be if Lennox convinced one of the passengers to ride with him.

Looking again at Andrea Gratham, Honor decided it would be best to leave things as they were. As she moved towards Horatio's rig, she found him no happier than she.

Before she could step up—Horatio made no move to help her—Lady Sarah called out. "Good heavens, Honoria, whatever are you doing with Horatio?"

As Honor could think of no answer to this, she looked to Lennox, who in turn scowled at his cousins.

"Can't have poor Mr. Duncan riding by himself," Hermione said primly, throwing back her head.

"Indeed?" Lady Sarah, likewise eyeing Lennox, slammed down her cane. "You two," she said, shaking the cane in Amanda and Pandora's direction, "go keep Horatio company."

"But-but," stammered Pandora, while Amanda stared balefully at the two phaetons approaching from behind.

"You've forgotten Foxley and Bellington," Richard volunteered, winking at the twins. "Can't have them riding alone either, now can we?"

"Iris can ride with Foxley, Hermione can go with Bellington," Lady Sarah said, turning again to the twins. "Hop to it, girls. The way Horatio handles a team, you're apt to miss the race."

The alacrity with which the Gratham twins responded was undoubtedly caused by the cane, but sheer infatuation drove the Pithnevel girls to obedience. Poor Foxley and Bellington, Honor thought.

"I suppose you've noticed Geoff is now by himself," Richard drawled.

"So he is," Lady Sarah said, glancing from Honor to Andrea. "Who shall volunteer to join him?"

Richard smiled. "Excellent move. Check and checkmate."

Andrea gazed up at him, baffled.

"Have you never noticed how my aunt maneuvers people about on her personal chessboard? She knows perfectly well I will never permit you to leave my side."

"Ah," said Miss Gratham as both turned to look at Honor.

Ah, indeed.

"Go along, Honoria." Lady Sarah nodded smugly. "Lennox does hate to be kept waiting."

Honor's face could not have been any more red as the earl helped her into his curricle, but Lennox seemed too busy muttering to notice. "Of all the manipulating, conniving . . ."

"Pray, try to understand. She means well—"

"Hermione has never meant well!" he exploded. "Torment me, that's what she means to do. Forcing herself and Iris upon our company, bullying her way into my curricle, and then having the utter gall to order Lolly back to the stables. . . ."

"Hermione?" Honor, realizing that he'd failed to notice Lady Sarah's manipulations, felt the most enjoyable relief. "But why would your cousin do such things?"

"Because of that accursed wage—— er, that is . . . it's just the way she is," Lennox finished lamely, staring straight ahead as he urged his team forward. He added a "contrary females," before lapsing into silence.

Gazing at his stiff profile as they rambled along, Honor

wished she could think of something clever to say. But
then, she thought uneasily, perhaps it was her talking yesterday that kept him intent upon the road now. Was he
keeping busy so she could not possibly burden him with
her confidences?

Even if he'd asked for those confidences, she should
know by now that in Polite Society, courtesy was often
used to conceal true feeling. His impeccable manners had
forced Lennox to show interest in her conversation; it did
not mean he'd enjoyed her babbling.

And my, how she had babbled. Whatever could she
have been thinking of, confiding in the man like that,
acting—no, feeling—as though he were someone she'd
known all her life?

Why can't you like me? she wondered as she gazed at
his handsome face. Not in the polite society way, but in a
sincere, caring fashion. She wished he could smile at her
and truly mean it.

"I can't see the others in this mob."

The words, as well as the abrupt fashion with which he
pulled the curricle to a halt, sent her thoughts scattering.
Unnerved that she could forget that the rest of their party
existed, Honor gaped at the crowd forming around them.

What must be most of London had gathered to watch
the race. Some strolled by as if this were Hyde Park at the
fashionable hour, while others did their mingling within
the comfort of their vehicles. Even should they manage to
locate the others, Honor realized, it would be no easy task
to join them in this circus of sight and sound.

Why this should bring a smile to her lips, she dared not
contemplate, but as she looked back to his lordship, she
discovered he wore one as well.

With a "harrumph" he turned away and jumped down.
"Might as well stay where we are," he offered in explanation. "I daresay my cousins will find us soon enough. For

the present, if you will excuse me, I'd like to inspect the undercarriage. My curricle is riding a bit queerly today."

Removing his coat and placing it on the seat, he reached for the rug on the floor. With a brief smile, he tossed it to the ground and lowered himself beneath the carriage.

Honor's gaze went to the coat. Without conscious thought, her hand stole out to touch it, finding that his warmth still clung to the blue superfine. Stripping free of her gloves, she sent a bare hand gliding across the heated surface.

"Ah, here you are, Miss Drummond."

She jumped two inches and her hand snapped back to her lap. "Fortesque! You startled me."

He looked from the coat to her hand and his smirk stretched from one side of his narrow face to the other. "I thought I might find you here," he purred. "I've brought this in case you've reconsidered making that wager."

"Ladies do not bet," Honor said in her most dampening tone as she eyed the book he held out to her.

"Coming from you, I find that a most unusual statement." He glanced at the coat before adding, "I remember a time when no man—be he baron *or* earl—could tell Honor Drummond what she might do."

"Times change, Fortesque. I believe Miss Drummond has repeatedly told you she does not wish to wager."

Honor started again, embarrassed to find Lennox had joined them. Glaring at Fortesque from the other side of the carriage, he grabbed his coat and replaced it on those solid shoulders. *Please don't let him have seen me touching it,* Honor prayed, flushing an absolute scarlet.

Not that either man noticed, being so busy facing off. "Speaking for the gal now, Stone? One would think you had something at stake here. A wager of your own, perhaps?"

Honor would have dismissed this as but another of Fortesque's meaningless taunts, had Lennox not gripped the sides of his vehicle with whitening knuckles, glanced quickly at Honor, and thereafter refused to meet her eyes.

"Ho there, Forty." Freddie Throckmorton ambled up to thump his back. "I'm told you've walked off with the betting book before I could . . ."

Honor lost the rest of the conversation. Wager? she was wondering. Could he mean their bet over who would own Lolly? But that had been a joke; Lennox couldn't actually want her dog. Could he?

But then, he had been so angry at Hermione for not letting Lolly tag along today. And he'd made every excuse why the dog should never go home to Drummond House. In all, there seemed something ominous in the fact that he and Lolly went everywhere together.

"Here they come!" Freddie shouted. A cloud of dust in the distance warned that the racers were fast approaching.

As was always the case, Honor soon forgot everything in the excitement of the competition. Standing up to watch, it felt as if she too rode on that track. Her heart pumped in the same wild rhythm as the thundering hooves, and she clenched her fists tightly, as if each squeeze could lend Mortimer that much more speed.

Oh, how she wished she could snatch the ribbons from his hands, for the inept fool was already lagging. She clasped her hands tighter, but Spencer drew ahead and Mortimer fell farther behind. Nothing she could do would stop Spencer; in dismay she watched him cross the line first.

She dropped back to the seat, feeling something wrench inside. Betting money had been such fun, but it felt rather awful to have lost her dog. She had to give him up—she could not renege—but what was she to do now without Lolly?

Swallowing painfully, she glanced at Lennox, hoping

for sympathy, but she instead found him being clapped on the back by Fortesque. Such sudden camaraderie was suspicious enough, but must it so obviously exclude her?

All at once, she felt hideously embarrassed for having stroked his empty jacket like a lovesick moonling. Confound that Lennox with his boyish grins and the charm he turned on and off at will. Oh, how he and Fortesque must be laughing at her. Foolish, gullible Honor, tricked into another wager.

Working her way into a proper dudgeon, she decided she'd been lured into this wager so they could make sport of her. All she had ever been to the ton was a diversion, she knew, a means of lightening their ennui. And Lennox, the epitome of what London had to offer, must find it vastly entertaining to take her only pet.

As Horatio Duncan drove up with the Gratham twins, with Lords Foxley and Bellington close on their heels, Honor wondered if everyone would arrive to witness her humiliation.

"Good show, eh what?" Horatio said to his fellow males, as if the ladies were not present. "I daresay Spencer has now set himself up as the man to beat."

"Spencer can't race his way out of a sack," Honor grumbled.

"Indeed?" With a patronizing smile, as if to say women-should-be-seen-but-not-heard, Horatio turned to Fortesque. "One might wonder how a female can speak with such authority on such masculine matters."

Hackles visibly rising, Honor assumed her own disdainful pose. "Perhaps because I twice beat the man myself. And, as I remember, I raced you to satisfaction as well, Mr. Duncan."

As the twins began to giggle, Horatio puffed up with offended dignity. Honor knew it was too bad of her to bring up that best-forgotten contest, but truly, the man was so tiresome, and how much should she be expected to bear?

"You cheated," Horatio blustered, pointing an accusing finger her way. "The challenge was with curricles," he whined. "This treacherous miss arrived in a phaeton."

Having forgotten that particular detail, Honor winced. "It was all I could find at such short notice."

"All you could steal, more like."

It was quite one thing to impugn her racing abilities, but to call her a liar, a cheat, and now a thief? "I had the general's permission, sir. But had I a curricle to race with, I still would have beaten you by considerable margin."

"Interesting." Fortesque, still clutching the betting book, stepped to the fore. "I don't suppose you'd be willing to back up your boast, Miss Drummond? If, say, we were to find you a curricle now?"

"You mean, race?" Horatio broke in, face as white as his ear-high cravat. "B-but, Forty, I am hardly dressed for such an occasion."

Fortesque sneered, as if doubting there could be any occasion for that puce-colored waistcoat. "Come, Duncan, you don't mean to let this brash young miss cast a slur upon us men? It's your masculine duty to show her no male can be bested on the racecourse."

"A race?" Freddie Throckmorton asked, his gambling instincts piqued. "But how famous. Hand me the betting book, Forty. I wish to place my money on Miss Drummond."

"Oh, dear," the Gratham twins blurted in unison. "Do something, Geoffrey."

Honor waited, holding her breath, thinking this was the moment of truth. If he stopped her, if he said anything to dampen the men's excitement, she would know he'd never meant to make sport of her.

But it was Fortesque who spoke first. "The twins are

right, of course. We men might better trust Lennox to teach the girl a lesson. Or is Miss Drummond afraid to challenge a whip of his lordship's stature?"

Teach the girl a lesson? Afraid to challenge? Not deigning to reply to such inflammatory words, Honor turned to Lennox. She wanted him to look at her, to talk to her, but he kept his gaze trained on Fortesque.

Hurt, and then angry, Honor picked up the reins. She would show them all that she was not some object to entertain them. If nothing else, she could at least win back her dog. "The same stakes, my lord," she bit out. "Only this time, Lolly shall be mine!"

And before Lennox could react, she was urging his horses free of the mob and hurrying off to the starting line. A quick glance backward revealed Lennox, grabbing for the betting book.

Only a fool would be surprised, she told herself as she coaxed the horses to more speed, and it would take an outright ninny to feel hurt.

Spurring his horses to fresh speed, she vowed that if his lordship craved amusement, she would give him all he could possibly want.

~13~

Amusement had to be the last thing on Geoff's mind.

When the twins had said "do something," he'd become more intent upon wrestling the betting book from Fortesque's hands than on preventing anything the headstrong Miss Drummond might do. As a result, he'd barely managed to move back before she could run his curricle over his foot.

Not that he could fault her reaction. Few gentlemen of his acquaintance could sit idly by in the face of such a deliberate taunt. Still, the fact remained that Miss Drummond was not a gentleman, and the consequences to her reputation could be dire indeed.

"Go get Lady Sarah," he told the twins. "Tell her Miss Drummond is . . ." he paused, noticing the gaze Fortesque gave them, ". . . that she's been taken ill."

"Ill?" everyone asked in varying degrees of incredulity.

"Er, yes. That was what she said to me just now. As she drove off. I cannot know the exact nature of her ailment, of course, only that she was quite anxious to reach home."

"Odd," Fortesque said with an annoying grin. "Same

ailment that felled her godmother yesterday, do you suppose?"

"I find it quite likely." Try as he might, Geoff could not keep the irritation from his tone. "Go on, girls. Be certain to tell Lady Sarah *all* that has transpired."

As they dashed off with Foxley and Bellington at their heels, Geoff reached for the betting book. Fortesque, who'd just begun to scribble in it, squawked out a protest. "I say, Stone, how unsporting of you."

"On the contrary. It is you who's unsporting. Or do you have Miss Drummond's leave to sign her name to that bet?"

Fortesque glared at him for a moment, but made no attempt to retrieve the book. With a shrug, for of course the damage was already done, Fortesque turned to converse with the steadily growing group of people around them.

Gritting his teeth, Geoff knew he could not stop the talk now; he could only hope to contain further gossip. He looked up at Horatio, who had yet to shut his jaw, and shouted, "Get down. I need your curricle."

Horatio was so startled by the command, he unthinkingly did as he was told.

Geoff could hear Fortesque clucking like an overfed hen. "Such haste, Stone? One must wonder why."

And you can keep wondering, he silently told Fortesque as he climbed into Horatio's carriage.

The feel of the reins touched off a new sense of urgency as he recalled how queerly his curricle had been acting, how he had been interrupted from his inspection. He could well imagine Miss Drummond, in her haste and anger, taking that last curve too tightly. . . .

He shook his head, banishing such thoughts. If he left at once, he should reach her in time.

But a hasty survey of Horatio's equipage warned that he

hadn't a prayer of catching anyone. The nags looked older than the dowager, and the carriage creaked ominously.

"Unseemly, this haste," Fortesque was saying to the crowd as Geoff coaxed the disreputable team forward. "One might think Lennox has something to hide."

In his urgency to be off, Geoff only half-heard the added, "The baron won't like this at all."

From her seat in her carriage, Lady Sarah looked down at the twins with maternal pride. Having recognized a crisis, they had come directly to her. Splendid chits. Thanks to their decisive action, the day could be salvaged.

"I say, shouldn't we go after Miss Drummond, too?" Pandy asked, looking back over her shoulder to the patiently waiting Bellington.

"Geoff will need our help," Amanda added with a longing gaze at Foxley.

"We can leave that to Richard." Lady Sarah smiled benignly, looking at both their young gentlemen. "Indeed, I think it best if you take Foxley and Bellington to explain things to the others."

"The four of us? Together?" As was often their way, the twins spoke in unison, their surprised delight mirrored in each identical feature.

"I wish it cast about that Honoria has been taken ill and I have gone home to tend her. I suppose you should see what you can do about finding rides home for Horatio and those dreadful Pithnevel girls, too. And," she added, waving her hand dismissively, "do not dally with those young beaux of yours. I expect you home in time for tea."

With a wide smile, proving they had no need for further encouragement, the twins went off with Foxley and Bellington. Sarah realized she had best start making matrimonial plans for them, the very moment their sister was wed to Richard. It would require managing, but then, managing was what she did best.

At the moment, however, her godchild was her first concern. Instructing her coachman to drive at once for Drummond House, she thought about the haste in which Lennox had gone after Honor. Perhaps rescuing her from some social disgrace was the very impetus the boy required.

She chuckled as the implications sifted through her brain. Yes indeed, she just might win their wager yet.

Marriage had to be the last thing on Geoff's mind. He was far too preoccupied in worrying over each curve he passed, and in feeling such dizzying relief when he failed to find that golden hair spilled upon the road.

He remained so bedeviled, in fact, that he barely heard the carriage rattling up behind him.

"Ah, Lord Lennox," a feminine voice cried out. "Is it true that most anyone can challenge you to a race?"

Looking over his shoulder, he found Andrea Gratham, sportily handling Richard's new curricle and pair. He reined in the nags, determined to make a quick exchange.

But when they had both stopped and he announced his intentions, Andy, as always, had other ideas. "The very devil," she said with a huff. "You're not going to race? And here I'd hoped to beat you at last."

It would serve the minx right if he answered her dare, Geoff thought. A good measure of his present skill could be contributed to the youthful competition Andy had provided in the back lanes, but London's elite had not been around to watch her commit such folly then.

"There will be no race," he announced as he took the ribbons from her hands. "You can't withstand the scandal and I am in too great a hurry to reach Miss Drummond."

"Are you indeed?" She tilted her head, eyeing him quizzically. "You needn't worry," she added more gently. "Richard is driving her home at this very moment. Or rather, she has the reins and Richard is no doubt biting his nails."

"Miss Drummond is driving?"

"She insisted." Taking advantage of his surprise, Andy regained the ribbons to hold them out of reach. "As do I."

"Be reasonable." With a shudder, he glanced back at Horatio's vehicle. "You can't expect me to travel in that."

"Tie those nags to a tree and ride to town with me."

He knew that look; he'd have to tie *Andy* to a tree before she'd relinquish the reins. Seeing no hope for it, he secured the horses—not that he thought they had the stamina to wander off—and returned to the other vehicle in a huff. No sooner did he sit than Andy was racing off down the road.

"From your speed," he said dryly, "I can only deduce that you planned to race in Miss Drummond's stead."

Without taking his eyes from the road—thank heavens, at this pace—Andy gave him a broad grin. "I did so want to see Fortesque's face when he saw it was me, and not poor Miss Drummond who bested you."

Geoff shook his head. Despite the flippancy, he knew what kindhearted Andy was about. Yet what was the sense in saving Miss Drummond, if it meant she must sit in the bumble broth instead? "A noble attempt, Andy girl, but London would have been bandying your good name about for weeks."

"They'd find another victim by tomorrow. Besides, you know I care nothing for gossip."

"Richard might."

"It bothers him less. Do stop pretending I made some grand sacrifice when we both know better. Little can happen with both Richard and the Fairbright name standing firm behind me. Poor Miss Drummond, on the other hand, has always stood quite alone."

With a pang, he realized Andy was right. He pictured Honor as she'd stood between her father and the baron, looking so lost and alone he'd felt compelled to ask her to dance.

Stop this, he told himself, appalled at the direction of his thoughts. "All well and good," he snapped, refusing to soften one whit, "but has anyone stopped to consider how Lady Sarah might react to such scandal?"

She began to giggle prettily. "Oh, Geoff, who do you think sent me?"

"Lady Sarah, the dowager countess of Fairbright, sent you to race in Miss Drummond's stead?"

"None other. I rather fancy she wished to see Fortesque's discomposure, too. She does so enjoy shaking things up."

"Yes, well," he said, unable to stop a chuckle of his own. Andy always could poke holes in his tirades, could get him to laugh at himself. "I suppose it does bear the dowager's stamp."

"In truth, I don't imagine she thought it would ever come to an actual race. Richard was to escort Miss Drummond home while I—" Andy's laughter stopped cold as she yanked on the ribbons. "I say," she said, her voice ringing with concern, "isn't that the two of them now?"

His gaze following her pointing finger, Geoff saw the wheel in the middle of the road, then the curricle tilted at an odd angle in the ditch. Remembering his earlier fears about the axle, he was jumping from the curricle before Andy could completely pull it to a halt.

∽14∽

"Wait," Richard said suddenly, ceasing his efforts, "do I hear horses?"

Honor, who'd been blowing the hair from her face after yet another mighty shove to dislodge the curricle, let out a sigh of relief. Stepping back from the vehicle, she sincerely hoped help was on the way. She did not mind the manual labor, but she did not like standing ankle deep in the cold mud.

Richard turned to listen, relinquishing his grip, and the curricle slid back to its original position. As this was a matter of inches, one could hardly fault the man for losing ground. Honor, who'd considered the case a hopeless one, sat on the side of the ditch, away from the vehicle. If rescue were at hand, she might better wipe the mud from her shoes.

But hearing the lilting laughter, she too turned her gaze to the road—just in time to witness Lennox driving up with Miss Andrea Gratham.

Honor tried to blame her sudden weakness on all that heaving, or even the shock sustained from the accident, but she feared something far more personal caused those wobbly knees. During their short drive, Richard had explained how Lennox had been trying to protect her good name, not goad her into tarnishing it, and she'd repaid the favor by crashing his curricle into a ditch.

"My God!" Lennox exclaimed as he leaped from the carriage. "Richard, where's—?"

"Relax, Geoff, your horses are fine. We tied them over there. Didn't think you'd want them wandering in the road."

Lennox nodded, but his gaze did not follow Richard's gesture. It found Honor, and there it stayed.

Like the silliest pea goose, she let herself imagine she saw concern, and no little relief. But that was before Miss Gratham's approach, drawing all attention instantly to her.

"Dear heavens, Richard," Andrea said, taking his hands in hers. "What happened? Are you hurt?" Seeing he was not, she spun to face Honor. "But poor Miss Drummond . . . quickly, Geoff, we need a rug; see how she is shivering."

"There's one in my curricle," Lennox said, turning at once. "I'll fetch it."

Showing little regard for her own discomfort, Miss Gratham trudged through the ditch to sit on the bank beside Honor. "You must be frightened half to death," she said, rubbing Honor's hands to warm them.

It was hard to hate a woman who was so confoundedly nice.

"Honor, frightened?" Richard, standing in the ditch before them, began to laugh.

"Only look at how pale she is."

"Nonsense. Like yourself, my dear, Honor would need a great deal more than this to bring her down."

Miss Gratham grinned. "Do you know, darling, this reminds me of another time we faced off in a ditch. Have you forgotten what I did to you then?"

"Not likely, my love. I never did manage to get the mud off that coat." Shaking his head, he turned to Honor. "She fell in. When I very nicely offered my arm, this vindictive miss yanked me into the ditch with her."

"Tell the truth, Richard. You were being beastly at the time. You quite deserved it."

"Did I? Odd, all I can remember about the incident is how it woke me to a great many things."

"Such as how you must never turn your back to me?"

"No. That I must never let you get away."

He gazed at his intended with such warmth, Honor could well imagine the scene. Lucky girl, Miss Gratham.

"Where is Geoff with that rug?" Andrea asked suddenly.

"I truly don't need it," Honor tried to protest, suspecting that Lennox was busy inspecting his beloved horses, but Richard had already gone scrambling after him.

Miss Gratham patted her hand. "Now that we are alone, let us dispense with the formality. I'd be ever more comfortable if I could use Honor and you'd call me Andy."

Honor looked down at her hands. "I feel dreadful about the inconvenience I've caused. You could be safely settled at home by now."

"And miss all the fun? Besides, I daresay I'd have done the same, with that ghastly Horatio goading me on."

"Truly?"

"You must not take him seriously. No one in the family ever does."

Honor tried not to smile. "I wish Lennox could share your sense of humor, but he'll be livid about his rig. Not that I blame him. I am too impulsive by half."

Andy squeezed her hands. "Do not fret. Geoff has never been one to hold a grudge. I've done a good deal worse, and he's always forgiven me."

That is because he's in love with you, Honor thought. "He—he doesn't like me overmuch," she said aloud.

"Nonsense. It certainly seems to me that he looks upon you quite fondly."

Honor shook her head. "He has never looked at me the way he looks at you."

Eyeing her speculatively, Andy rose. "An interesting theory. Perhaps we should test it. Shall we join the gentlemen now and see who Geoff gazes at first?"

When she would demure, Andy tugged her along. A hundred butterflies fluttered in Honor's stomach, but Lennox proved too busy inspecting his vehicle to glance at either girl.

"Odd, isn't it?" he said to Richard.

"Axle's snapped," was Richard's verdict, his face likewise troubled as he bent over to scrutinise the damage.

"Then fix it," Andy told them. "We must have Miss Drummond home before the baron comes looking for her."

Lennox looked at Honor then, but he did so with a scowl. "Then take her home in the other carriage."

"Me?" Andy said, fluttering her lashes. "Hardly proper, dear Geoff, to set two feeble females out upon the road by ourselves."

"You're getting as manipulative as my aunt," Richard teased with a grin. "But I daresay you are right. Geoff, why don't you escort the ladies home? I can stay here until you return with help."

"Please, deal with the horses first," Honor interrupted. "I've caused inconvenience enough as it is. After all, it isn't as if I've a prayer of escaping notice now. At this hour, half the town will be out on the streets."

"Here, you can wrap up in my bonnet and pelisse," Andy said, removing them and thrusting the bundle into Honor's hands. "And do not argue, Richard. I have no intention of leaving you here by yourself."

"Stubborn female. You do know that I should order you home, but I find I am very much anxious for the company." He reached for her, placing a protective arm about her shoulder. "But this plan of yours, darling? Don't you think trying to pass Honor off as yourself pulls up a bit lame?"

She shrugged. "Most people see what they expect to see and from a distance, she looks enough like me. Besides, if anyone should spot Honor, Geoff can always put it about that we found her wandering home. That it was her 'illness' that caused this accident with the curricle."

The men exchanged concerned glances. "It might be the very thing," Richard told Lennox, looking back to the broken axle. "Far better than to have the truth come out."

"The truth?" Andy asked, looking from one to the other.

"Er, yes. About the race." Lennox looked at his vehicle. "We're trying to spare Miss Drummond's reputation, after all." He inhaled, as if coming to a decision, and then turned with a frown to Honor. "Come, we must get you home."

Honor felt he could as easily have said, "We must be rid of you." Climbing up beside him in the curricle, she braced herself for the long and miserable ride home.

For what in truth could she say to the man? Sorry, I thought you meant to make sport of me? I repaid you in kind by destroying your rig? No, whatever she said would only make matters worse.

"What precisely happened?"

Honor blurted out the first thing that came into her mind. "I, er, lost my composure, I suppose. Mr. Duncan was being dreadful and I—"

"Not then. Later. With the curricle."

"Oh, you mean our accident? Why, I don't precisely know. One moment we were tooling along, and then I felt a jolt, a snap really, and the next thing I knew, we were bumping out of control and into that ditch."

"Richard tells me you could both have been killed, had you not handled things so skillfully."

Sensing his grudging admiration, she blushed. "My riding tutor was often, well, he had a fondness for brandy. My lessons were always an adventure."

He looked at her oddly and she wished she had not spoken. When would she learn that no gentleman wished to hear about her unorthodox upbringing?

"Richard also said you dealt quite ably with my horses. I suppose one of your father's staff was a veterinarian?"

"Sergeant Potts. I can assure, my lord, that your animals have come to no serious harm."

"Hang the horses, what about you, Miss Drummond? Don't you realize you could have been killed?"

His outburst stunned them both. Honor edged as far back as the seat would allow, and he retreated into silence. She could sense that something uneasy hovered between them, but since she could not guess its cause, she assumed—as was invariably the case—that she must be at fault.

"We're almost in town," he said abruptly. "Put on the bonnet and see if we can't scrape through this unscathed."

Obediently, she tied the strings of the bonnet and drew the borrowed shawl close around her shoulders. Lennox stared with deliberate intent at the road ahead.

As they drew up to the same curb they had stopped at yesterday, Honor's misery grew. How foolish she felt now, remembering her hopes for today's outing. How naive, to wish for a future with this man.

"It was our bet," she forced out. She wanted things settled between them, in case she never saw him again. "That's why I did it."

He looked at her as if she'd spoken in Chinese.

"I couldn't bear to give up Lolly. I know I talk a great deal about finding him a new home, but I never stop hoping some miracle will keep him with me. When Spencer finished first, and you won him in our bet, I went a little insane, I think. I never truly meant to ruin your curricle." Her voice broke and she struggled to keep it even. "I'm sorry, I've made a monstrous mess of things."

He looked at her, long and hard. "I was never serious about our bet. Good heavens, I don't need a dog."

It should have made her feel better, having this confirmed, but in truth, she only felt worse. How he must hate her, though surely, no more than she detested herself. "I must go in," she said brokenly, turning away. "The baron will be angry enough about this."

He grabbed for her wrist, forcing her to look at him. "If anything goes wrong," he said quickly, like a boy anxious to complete an unpleasant task, "I want you to know, there are alternatives to returning to Scotland. For you and your dog."

"I beg your pardon?"

"Confound it. Had I not suggested the outing, you would not be in this situation. If there is any unpleasantry, well, the least I can do is offer my name."

Honor could only stare at him, surprise rendering her speechless. What an absolutely noble—though admittedly reluctant—offer.

"I will leave now," he said, hopping down to help her from the carriage, "but I shall call on you later this afternoon to see how you fare. I can say I am inquiring after your health."

Honor nodded, still somewhat stunned, and more than a little flustered by the touch of his hand. Even when she was safely on her feet, she could not bring herself to relinquish his grasp. He gazed at her, no less bemused, and for a wonderful moment, she could feel a tug between them, as if he too felt a need to move closer.

He looked away first, clearing his throat and swiftly removing his hand. Honor mumbled some nonsense about a need for haste, and his agreement was distressingly enthusiastic.

Seeing no help for it, she made her way to the slit in the back hedge. She turned once, wanting one last glimpse of him, but Lennox was already driving off.

If anything goes wrong, he had said. Still tingling where his hand had covered her own, Honor told herself no, that it would be utterly wretched to take advantage of his generosity.

Yet oh, what temptation. She could make him happy, given time and opportunity. Perhaps she could even convince him to fall in love.

And in all, she could think of a great many ways that things could yet go wrong.

❧ 15 ❧

Lady Sarah sat in the Drummond drawing room, watching the abigail pour her tea. A good girl, this Betsy—had Honoria's best interests at heart. Together, they might just scrape through this fiasco yet.

As the front bell chimed, Sarah stiffened. Barely an hour had passed; did the gossipmongers now travel as quickly as the rumors they spread?

"Miss Drummond is indisposed at the moment," she heard Rawlings announce. "Perhaps you can call again tomorrow?"

Unjust, that a dolt like Drummond should have such obliging servants. Her own butler forever required detailed instructions, but Rawlings need only be told, "protect your mistress" to set about barring the house to unwanted guests.

"Ah, but I assure you, Miss Drummond will see me." Overbearingly smug, von Studhoff's voice grew louder as he apparently pushed past into the house. "Tell her I shall await her in the drawing room."

Appalled by the man's arrogance—and the fact that he'd soon be disturbing her—Sarah declined the teacup with a

wave of her hand. What utter gall, forcing his way into another's home; the boorish lout begged for a setdown. Rising to her feet, Sarah decided she was the very one to give
it to him.

"Actually," he said suddenly, "tell Miss Drummond to
wait. I wish to speak to the general first. Alone."

A private interview with Drummond? How curious.
With a grin, Betsy nodded to the door to their right, as if
to imply that Sarah might wish to eavesdrop on her host.

To others, this might be the most cardinal of sins, but
Sarah had no thought to spare for Drummond's sensi-
bilities—if indeed he had any. She knew only that she
must hear what was discussed, as it could be crucial to
Honor's future.

With a conspiratorial grin, the quick-thinking abigail
picked up the tea tray and led the way through the connecting door. Sarah had barely cleared the frame when von
Studhoff burst into the room behind them. "I will have
tea," he demanded as he crossed the room. "And be quick
about it!"

Sarah might have lingered by the door, had Betsy not
gestured to an alcove behind the draperies. It was fortunate
that they hid, for moments later, watching from behind the
drapes, Sarah saw von Studhoff duck his head through the
door. He glanced briefly about the room, and then smiled
with satisfaction as he shut the door firmly behind him.

Curious and curiouser.

As they left their hiding place, Betsy looked down at the
tray, then grinned at the connecting door. From the twinkle
in the maid's eye, Sarah realized Betsy meant to serve the
untouched cup to the baron. Not to save herself the extra
trip to the kitchen, but to annoy that Bavarian bully by
serving him cold tea.

Hating to miss a moment of this, Sarah set her ear
against the connecting door. Odd, how von Studhoff had

checked the room. It would seem whatever he had to say to Drummond, he did not want overheard.

Sarah smiled. All the more reason, she was convinced, that she must listen in.

General Drummond scurried down the hallway, feeling unhappy about the way he rushed to obey the baron's summons. Lord knew, he had enough else to occupy his time, between this mission for Pithnevel, and the alarming news his man of business had just imparted, yet here he was running, merely because the baron beckoned. It was not what Drummond wished to do, but alas, beggars rarely possessed the luxury of choice.

And a beggar was precisely what he'd soon be. According to his man of business, his finances had worsened in the past few days, despite the baron's advice and his loan of a few hundred pounds. As Drummond considered the astronomical sum quoted, he shuddered. Even were he to pawn everything he owned, he could not come close to settling the blunt. Should the baron become upset and withdraw his support, it was debtor's prison for him. It was utter ruin.

"Here you are at last!" From his scowl, it was clear the baron was not in a good mood. Of all the ill timing, Drummond thought with a sinking sensation—now what could his daughter have done to displease the man?

"Forgive the delay," he said, trying not to stammer, "but I-I was with my man of business. I, er, have certain details to deal with before I can leave town."

"Oh?" The dark eyes widened with interest; the baron all but pinned him with his gaze. "Leaving us, are you? A bit sudden, isn't it? No emergency, I hope."

"Er, no. Mere business." A blatant lie, but no one must know the true details of his mission. Not even his own flesh and blood could be told. "Would you like something to drink?" he asked to change the subject. "I can order tea."

"Do not bother." The baron's gaze dropped disdainfully to the tray on the table. "I do wish you would train your servants properly. This tea was inexcusably cold by the time it reached my lips."

Drummond allowed himself a small sigh of relief. This was a minor irritation and readily remedied. Had Honor's behavior been at fault, the solution might not be so simple. "Terribly sorry," he said as he stretched for the bellpull. "Here, let me ring for another pot."

"Do not bother. I have lost my taste for it."

The man continued to scowl, Drummond noted as he let his hand fall uselessly to his side. His relief, it would seem, had been premature.

As if realizing that his reply had been abrupt, at best, the baron tried a smile. "It is quite all right, my friend, I have not come to be entertained. I am here out of concern for you. My sources warn that your financial situation has grown grim. This sudden business trip you spoke of—is it perhaps a last, desperate attempt to set things aright?"

Drummond had the overwhelming urge to tell him the truth, that only another, more substantial loan could save him, but that would sacrifice his alibi for the mission. A soldier first and foremost, Drummond would not let the lure of money lead him to betray the country he served. "In a manner of speaking" was all he could think of to say.

"But perhaps this trip would not be necessary," the baron said with the smile of a parent with a wayward child. "If I were to settle these, er, embarrassments . . ."

Hope sprang to life in Drummond's chest, but he reined himself in. "I couldn't allow—"

"Nonsense. Caring about Honoria as I do, could I allow her only parent to suffer such worry and strife? No, I am afraid I must insist. The very moment Honoria and I are wed, dear friend, I shall make certain your creditors never dun you again."

Just like that, his worries were gone? Drummond had the sudden absurd urge to kiss the baron, right on top of his shiny bald head.

"So you see, General, there is no need, now, for you to go away."

There was, of course, but he could scarce tell the baron the true reason why. "Actually, there is. My creditors will not wait forever. I must stall them, convince them to wait until after the wedding."

The baron's gaze held a considering gleam. "I see. But what of Honoria? Where is she to stay while you are gone?"

"She's to go to Pithnevel House." At the man's frown, Drummond hurried on defensively. "Only place I could find, on such short notice. Lady Sarah's home is filled to the brim with Gratham chits."

"But Lennox will be hovering about." The baron frowned. "Is that gazetted rake the sort of influence we wish for our sweet, innocent Honoria?"

Drummond, who'd been relieved to have his daughter settled, would not have quibbled were Casanova himself camped at the house. Yet now, with all the baron's questions, he began to feel uneasy.

Von Studhoff pressed on. "I cannot like this. That rogue will fill her impressionable mind with unwarranted hopes. He will have his diversion, then feel no guilt at waltzing away. Honoria is too guileless to see his true character, but you and I, General, we are men of the world. We know that no earl will stoop to marriage with a mere soldier's daughter."

Drummond, wincing at this reference to his humble

start, felt his resentment revive. Lennox—that cad—meant to trifle with his girl? If he broke Honor's heart . . .

Drummond stopped himself. Odd, this sudden surge of parental feeling.

"Nor, I regret to add," the baron went on, his face a study of concern, "would Lennox ever feel the need to ease *your* burden. Such a gambler will have too many of his own debts to offer funds for yours."

Too true, Drummond thought glumly. But then, he had always known the baron was his only hope.

"I am not by nature a man of impulse," the baron added, "but how can I stand by and watch the woman I love be needlessly hurt by some libertine's thirst for diversion? We both know Honoria is impulsive, given to rash actions. What if she should take it into her head to run off one night, leaving me as she did poor Wharton?"

Drummond could hear his own gulp. What indeed? A man as proud as von Studhoff would have no choice but to cry off. The baron would march away and never come back, leaving him with an unmarriageable daughter and insurmountable debt.

"In truth, I can see but one way out of our dilemma," the baron said firmly. "The sole way to keep Lennox away from Honoria is to place her beneath my care. I suggest our wedding be held at once."

"At once?"

"Ah, splendid, I knew you would agree." The baron beamed at him, as if Drummond had learned a new trick. "I shall procure a special license and we can have the ceremony the day after tomorrow. You should be home from . . . just where was it you said you meant to go?"

"Here and there." This time, Drummond didn't mean to be deliberately vague; he was too dazed to think of a more suitable answer. Logically, he knew the baron was right, that this was the best solution for everyone, but some deep, buried part of him sensed that all was not quite as it should be. "Sunday is impossible," he said, half because it was, yet half because he felt the need to stall. "I might not be able to return for a week or more."

Von Studhoff raised a brow. "Then we shall set the date for Sunday next. Surely you share my desire for haste? The sooner Honoria and I are wed, after all," he added with a broadening smile, "the sooner I can discharge your debts."

How neatly things had fallen into place, Drummond tried to tell himself. All would be soon settled splendidly—his debts, his daughter's future, everything. "A week from Sunday," he echoed feebly. "I-I'll speak to Lady Pithnevel. She's offered to help with the social side of things."

Smiling with that same paternal favor, the baron strolled up to grasp his shoulders. "Then all that is left is to inform Honoria. I trust you shall see to it at once?"

"Yes. Yes, of course."

"Good." Abruptly releasing his shoulders, von Studhoff clicked his heels and marched from the room. "Tell her I shall return later this evening," he flung out as he passed through the door, "to escort her to the opera."

"Won't be here," Drummond called out to him. "Chit should be settled into Pithnevel House by then."

But the baron was already gone and Drummond found he hadn't the spirit to go after him. No matter. Von Studhoff would learn Honor's location soon enough, and by then, hopefully, Drummond would already be on his way to the coast.

He was relieved—he truly was—to have so much settled so satisfactorily. Retrieving information from their scouts in France would be dangerous enough; it was good to be freed of distractions over the future. From now on, his girl would have her baron to take care of her. They were lucky to have found a man like von Studhoff. They should both be ecstatic.

Given time, he could easily convince himself. The trick, he feared, would be in convincing his daughter.

Honor was tiptoeing to the stairs, intent upon reaching her bedroom without discovery, when her godmother crept out of the salon in front of her. "Whatever are you doing?" Honor whispered, infected by her ladyship's stealth.

"One might better ask what *you* have been doing all this time," the old woman hissed back. "Quick, up to your room. Your father is soon on his way to talk to you."

"He knows about the race?"

"That is the least of our problems. Go on; I shall explain later." Her godmother's gaze slid to the drawing room. "I shall try to stall him, but do hurry."

Honor raced up the stairs, turning into the hallway even as she heard Lady Sarah greet her father. Their discourse was brief—they'd never been on the best of terms—but her godmother managed to convey that Honor had been unexpectedly taken ill and had gone to her room to recover.

Grinning, amazed to find an ally in Lady Sarah, Honor hurried to her room. She managed to hop into bed before she heard the knock at the door. Yanking the covers to her chin, she called out to her father to enter the room.

She tried to steady her breathing as he approached, a bit daunted by the scowl on his face. "Not feeling the thing, I'm told," he began, making it seem more an accusation than an offer of sympathy.

"I imagine it was the heat." She brushed a hand over her cheeks, knowing they must be suitably flushed from her recent exertion. "I am feeling somewhat better now."

"Good."

His relief was so vocal, she wondered if he had actually

been concerned about her. Warmed by the thought, Honor began to reassure him further, but he cut her off by announcing curtly that he was leaving this afternoon on business.

"Leaving," she sputtered. "But where? And what of me? It is not at all the thing for me to stay here alone."

"I've made arrangements for you to go to Pithnevel."

Her first impulse was to protest—every sensibility rebelled at the prospect of Iris and Hermione's company for an extended period of time—but as she remembered that Lennox was residing there, she could see intriguing possibilities.

As if he too were considering them, the general cleared his throat. "Your stay shall be of short duration," he said stiffly. "In less than a fortnight, you shall be setting up your own establishment."

"My own what?"

"Yes indeed." The general beamed with forced joviality. "The baron and I have settled upon your wedding date."

Honor gripped the covers, choosing her words with care. "Settled? Papa, do let's stop and consider this. In truth, isn't a baron—and a foreign one at that—aiming a bit low? We're at war—we should ally ourselves with an Englishman."

"For lud's sake, girl, you have already agreed to this betrothal. It is far too late to be crying off now."

There was a tic over the general's right eye, a sure warning that his patience was stretched, but Honor, hearing the words "too late," knew only her own desperation. "We must think this over carefully," she pressed. "A baron is so ... so mundane. A viscount, or perhaps an earl, would make more sense."

"Not a bit of it. A baron in the hand is worth a dozen earls in the bush."

"But what if he had the title *and* a prominent name?

Rather like, say, someone of"—she hesitated, tried her best to sound casual—"Lennox's position. A man like that could lead our way into any drawing room in London."

"The only place Lennox plans to lead us is into ruin."

Honor bit her lip. This was not going at all well. "You cannot know such a thing."

"All London knows the man is a gambler," the general erupted, his eyes flashing with anger. "How is it you alone know otherwise? What has he done to prove he is anything more than a dissolute rake?"

Honor thought of how Lennox had protected Lolly, but knew better than to mention that to her father.

"Has he declared an undying love? You're deluding yourself, girl, if you think he means to do more than enjoy himself at your expense. He will never offer love."

Thinking of his offer—albeit halfhearted—Honor felt her own anger ignite. "Since when is love a necessity? As I recall, you scoffed quite liberally when I mentioned it."

"Stop spinning moonbeams, girl. Why can't you be happy with the baron?"

"Happy?" Sitting up, Honor thought she might burst. "You're the one spinning moonbeams. If anyone means to enjoy himself at our expense, it is your precious baron."

The tic above his eyes twitched ominously. "You don't know what you're saying."

"Don't I? Have you never noticed how cold he is, how condescending?"

"As ever, child, you let your imagination run wild. The man is my friend."

"Is he?" She rose to her knees, desperation getting the best of her. "Friends don't sneer when they talk to you— they rush to your aid when you need them. Can you truly imagine the baron ever bestirring himself on our account? Can you?"

"Just who do you think offered to bail me out of debt?"

"Debt?" Honor sat back on her feet, the wind knocked out of her. "Are matters that bad that you must be 'bailed' out?"

Drummond seemed to crumple as he saw the horror on his daughter's face. "My situation is impossible," he explained feebly. "Von Studhoff is my only hope."

"So you sold me." She shook her head slowly, the implications settling in. "You used your only child to pay off your debts."

"No!" As if that outburst had taken his last bit of strength, the general eased himself down to sit on the bed. He spoke to the wall, as if unable to face her. "The baron is solid and responsible, and well, to be honest, I have always felt that you needed a guiding hand. I truly believe he cares about you, child."

He might have tried to smile, but since Honor could see only half his face, it could well be a grimace instead. "It is because of this love for you that he offered to pay my blunt. And in all candor, I shudder to think what will become of us should he not."

"But there must another way. A loan, perhaps. I could talk to Lennox—"

"Lennox has his own sizeable stack of vouchers," he broke in lifelessly, defeat in every line of his body. "He is hardly about to take on more. Only a man blinded by love could overlook the extent of my debt."

Honor winced. No, not even in her wildest dreams could she delude herself that far. If the earl's offer had seemed reluctant this morning, how much less enthusiastic he would be when he learned what a liability she and her father posed.

"Someone must soon cover my losses," the general went on, "or they shall be carting me off to debtor's prison. You are my sole hope, child. You and this marriage."

Honor tried to speak, but could not. She tried to swallow but couldn't manage that either. Everything inside seemed frozen, paralyzed by the looming prospect of a lifetime with the baron.

She watched her father's hand rise, as if he meant to reach out to her, but it hovered only a moment, trembling slightly, before falling uselessly back to the bed.

"In truth, you have every right to refuse," he said, his voice barely audible as he continued to speak to the wall. "I know I have never been a proper parent. I tried my best, I honestly did, yet each time I looked at you, each time I saw your dear mother smiling back at me, it was all I could do not to scream at the loss. I am not good at handling grief—it always seemed easier to just run away."

"Oh, Papa."

He sighed heavily, as if to collect himself, and then rose to his feet. "I just want you to know that I would not ask for your help if things were less crucial."

"I know." She bit her lip to keep it from trembling. Deep inside, a small voice cried out that she must refuse, that she could not tie herself to the baron, not when there was even the slightest chance that she might be with Lennox instead.

Moonbeams. That was what the general called her hopes, and how could she argue? At best, Lennox had treated his offer as a sacrifice on his part. And she loved him too much, she realized, to ever force him to make it.

She looked at the general, stubbornly facing his wall. How difficult this was for him. All her life, she had dreamed of the moment her father would turn to her, and now here he was, begging for her help.

She had to give it. Else how could she live with herself afterward?

"Do not fret," she told him, struggling to keep her tone

airy and light. "I was teasing. I shall marry the baron whenever you wish."

He went slowly to the door, still refusing to look at her. "God help me, but you still remind me too much of your mother," he said softly as he quit the room.

∽16∾

"Look here," Richard said softly, no doubt hoping to prevent Andy from hearing. "I hope I am wrong, but doesn't it appear that your axle has been tampered with?"

Geoff looked up from his inspection, his friend's concern mirrored in his features. Richard was right. The ordinary axle did not split in so cleanly a fashion.

"But, Richard," Andy said behind them, her own face a study in alarm, "you cannot mean . . ." She broke off, as if the thought were too awful to utter aloud.

"I didn't want you involved in this."

Geoff shrugged. "She's not apt to turn squeamish, nor to leave off badgering, so she might as well hear it all."

Andy smiled with determination. "Which is?"

Richard's own face remained grim. "We must wait for confirmation, but it would seem someone deliberately sawed through that axle."

"But why? And who? Geoff hasn't an enemy in the world."

Unless one considered Fortesque, Geoff thought. Yet why bother to damage a curricle the man could gain by winning their wager? And it was difficult to imagine Fortesque with either the brains or courage to manage attempted murder.

Murder? Preposterous. Brought an ugly taste to the mouth, that word.

Richard looked again at the axle. "Perhaps Geoff has no enemies, but remember, he was not alone in the curricle."

"Honor?" She shook her head, frowning. "But who would wish to harm such a delightful girl?"

As if he'd swallowed that ugly taste, Geoff felt the uneasiness squirm in his gut. Eyeing the other carriage, he made up his mind. "My man should be along momentarily. Would you mind waiting while I take this vehicle?"

"Not at all, but why—"

But Geoff had already hopped in the curricle and taken up the reins. All at once, he found he could not reach the Drummond town house soon enough.

Honor huddled into the wing chair before the fire, listening to the baron's tirade with growing dismay. Was this what her life was to be, a lifetime of never-ending lectures about what she must and must not do?

I can bear this, she insisted silently as he droned on about the proper respect for the position to which he would elevate her. She must bear it, she told herself; it was the only way to save her poor father.

She thought of how weary the general seemed as he rode off today. It worried her that he'd left in such haste; she prayed that whatever he meant to do, he would be safe.

Looking about the huge, unfamiliar library, she tried not to feel homesick, but how would she get through the next few days here at Pithnevel House? His lordship and Lady Maude seemed nice, but Hermione and Iris could prove a trial. How quick they'd been to inform her that Lennox was banished from the house for the length of her stay, how happy to relate that he was now residing in less desirable quarters above the stable.

This too was for the best, she tried to tell herself. Were she to bump into Lennox often, her hard-won composure was certain to break.

"Why are you still sitting here?" the baron broke into her thoughts.

She could only look at him blankly. Mind racing, she tried to remember what he expected, but it was hopeless. She simply had not been paying attention.

Leaning against the mantel, he clicked open his watch and frowned. "We have less than an hour if we hope to arrive at the opera before the curtain rises."

"Opera? But I cannot possibly go out tonight. I told you, I took ill this morning at the outing with Lady Sarah. She told me I must rest."

"Nonsense. We must show these pasty-faced English my future wife is made of sterner stuff."

Again her mind raced, trying to find some escape. Soon enough she'd be forced to spend her life with this man; she deserved at least this one evening to herself.

All at once, Lennox burst through the door like a knight charging to the rescue. He seemed harried as his eyes sought her out, but once his gaze settled upon Honor, every inch of him seemed to relax.

Stunned by his entry—though no less delighted—Honor could only gape at him, her heart fluttering madly. How handsome he was, and how dashing beside the staid and proper baron.

"Do you mind, Lennox?" the baron spouted as he stepped behind her to set a proprietary hand on her shoulder. "This is a private conversation between Miss Drummond and myself."

As Lennox strode forward, the pressure on her shoulder increased. He frowned, a question in his eyes, but mindful of her father's dilemma, Honor forced herself to look away.

"I came to see how she fared." As if seeing her evasion and taking a cue from it, Lennox assumed a formal tone. "She was not feeling at all the thing when I last saw her."

So he had remembered his offer to inquire after her health. Honor could not control a tiny smile.

The baron made a clicking sound with his tongue. "Is it any wonder she is ill, considering the unsavory element you exposed her to? What were you thinking of, involving such a sensitive miss in such outings?"

"Come now, von Studhoff, the afternoon was very properly chaperoned by Lady Sarah."

"Indeed," the baron scoffed. "She should know better than to bring someone of Miss Drummond's delicate nature to such an event. There was racing, was there not? And betting books being bandied about?"

"How did you—"

"I never noticed," Honor interrupted, wanting such line of questioning stopped at once. Her eyes pleaded with Lennox, begging him not to reveal the truth. Were the baron to learn how close she had come to betting—and racing as well—he might yet cry off. "I was ill, you must realize."

Looking from her to the hand on her shoulder, Lennox frowned. As his gaze returned to her own, his gray eyes again asked a silent question. She wanted so much to say, yes, please rescue me, but she was not so wretchedly selfish, she could forget her father's troubles. "The baron is right about the outing," she said instead, trying to sound gay. "He generally is about these things. Indeed, it might be wiser if I stayed at home from now on."

The hand left her shoulder. As the baron strutted across the room, Lennox continued to gaze at her. Fearing she might cry, Honor again looked away.

"You can leave us now," the baron commanded from the other side of the room. "Do hurry and dress."

"But I—"

"Must you argue?" Von Studhoff gave her his patented frown. "We will be late enough for the opera as it is."

"Opera?" Lord Pithnevel appeared at the opened doorway. "My dear Honor, as much as I would like to indulge you, no decent guardian would allow you to go out this evening. No indeed, I must insist that you run upstairs this moment and bundle yourself in for the night. Perhaps if you are feeling more the thing, you can visit the opera tomorrow."

Honor looked to the baron, certain he would insist, but though he glowered at Lennox, he seemed loathe to confront Pithnevel. "I had not realized the poor girl was so ill," von Studhoff said smoothly, as if she had not been telling him so for the past hour and more. "You should have spoken up, my dear. It is simple enough to change our plans."

How reasonable he sounds, Honor thought, watching the man smile pleasantly at Pithnevel. No wonder her father wished her to wed him—he'd been spared the baron's lectures.

Having no wish to endure another one, she took the reprieve Pithnevel offered and said yes, perhaps it was as well that she retired for the night. With a quick curtsey, she left the room before the baron could change his mind.

She did not see, in her hurry to be off, how fiercely Lennox was frowning behind her.

Pithnevel noticed. Trying not to grin, for he had never seen Geoff in such a dither, he began the process of removing his uninvited guest. It would require all his diplomatic skill—he could ill afford to alienate the baron—yet he'd no desire to sit down to dinner with him, either.

"Ah, Geoffrey," he said, turning to his startled nephew. "We need to go over the details of that project I've asked you to oversee. Can you spare a few moments?" The "project" was sheer fabrication. He could only hope Geoff would guess his intent and the baron would take the cue to leave.

Geoff gave a quick nod, being quick on the uptake, but the baron remained obtuse. "Now see here," the man protested, "I cannot like the thought of a randy buck like Lennox in the same quarters as my intended. It would be more appropriate should he repair to his club for the duration of her stay."

"But I am not in the same quarters!"

Though amused by his nephew's pique, Pithnevel sent him a cautioning frown. "Geoff is staying in the gentleman's suite above the stables. I need him close. We'll be conferring constantly."

Von Studhoff went wooden, drawing himself up to his full six and a half feet. "I suppose that must do," he said with a telltale tightening of his jaw. "After all, her stay will be brief, with our wedding taking place on Sunday next."

Geoff stared at him openmouthed.

"Drummond did speak of this to you, did he not?" the baron went on, sparing a smirk for Geoff. "I would so like your help with the arrangements."

With a grunt, and without another word, Geoff quit the room. Interesting, his reaction. One might be inclined to think his nephew did not wish this wedding to take place.

Whatever Geoff's inclinations, however, his exit managed what might have taken an hour or more of diplomacy. As if he'd come for the sole purpose of riling Geoff, the baron made his excuses and was soon out the door.

Loathsome man. Taunting Geoff with his news, then taking great pleasure when he stomped from the room.

But Sunday next? Pithnevel stroked his chin. Why, he wondered, was there need for such haste?

This would bear careful watching.

Lolly yapping at his heels, Geoff strode across the straw-covered stable floor. He was so overset at the moment, the only thing that could calm him was grooming his horses.

He'd removed his jacket and set it on a peg before he remembered his animals had yet to arrive. Still, good hard work was what he needed at the moment, so he grabbed a brush and set to work tending to his uncle's horses instead.

He felt like an utter dolt. Racing to Miss Drummond, only to find her already moved to his uncle's establishment, then charging up to Pithnevel House to spot that ostentatious carriage parked outside.

Worry had gone to irritation, then outrage as he watched the baron at work. What was wrong with Miss Drummond that she would so meekly accept such abuse? Geoff had itched to tell the man exactly what transpired this morning, how that "sensitive miss" had stolen his curricle— anything that would remove her from the brute's oppressive control.

But then she had looked at him, stopping him dead with those expressive eyes, reminding him of the one rabbit he'd managed to snare as a child. He could still see its tiny limbs quivering as he wavered between snapping its neck or letting it hop away. In the end, Geoff had released that silly hare, just as he had Honor Drummond.

Confound it, but if she was so intent upon having her baron, what was left for him to do?

For a moment, he thought he might have voiced the question aloud, since Lolly seemed to bark out an answer. Looking up though, he saw it was excitement the dog meant to convey, the sheer joy of being reunited with its mistress.

At the stable door, Miss Drummond smiled weakly as she bent down to stroke the dog's back. Geoff, struggling not to follow in Lolly's footsteps, ruthlessly denied that he too felt pleasure in seeing her there.

"The baron has left," she said, her voice as flat as a puddle of month-old champagne.

Of course the brute was gone; she would never dare come here, else. Yet watching her—confound it, he could not make himself look away—Geoff found it increasingly difficult to maintain his wrath.

She stood in the doorway, an actress awaiting her cue, prepared either to take a step forward, or to melt back into the darkness of the night.

Oh, yes, she was quite like his rabbit. Soft, vulnerable, and twice as elusive. Her big, wide eyes cried out to him, but only a fool would answer. No man could rescue a woman who was forever running away.

"I just wished to thank you," she went on, her voice strained. "For not telling the baron what happened. He would have been livid, had he learned the truth."

"As far as I can see, the man is always livid."

A smile flickered briefly on her lips. "Still, I am grateful that you said nothing to jeopardize this marriage."

Ah yes, this marriage. Geoff felt more than ever the dolt. What was wrong with him, standing here mooning like some lovestruck boy and overlooking the wedding of Sunday next? "I cannot see that I did you a favor," he said stiffly, applying himself once more to his brushing.

Biting her lip, she looked away. "To me it was a very great favor. I only wish I could repay you in kind."

Then don't marry the man, he nearly blurted, but he told himself it was no affair of his what the chit chose to do with her life. No affair of his at all.

She continued to stand there, saying nothing, no doubt hoping he'd take up the conversational slack. Geoff, who hadn't the slightest idea what to say, grew more annoyed.

As if wishing to spare the animal his ungentle brushing, she spoke out softly. "I don't want you to think I'm ungrateful. I will never forget all you have done for me. You have been a good friend."

Friend? Odd, but that word rankled. "It sounds as if you're about to say good-bye," he snapped. "What is afoot, do you mean to run off again?"

"No," she said, so softly he almost did not hear. "Running away, I've learned, solves nothing."

And then, with the consistency for which her sex was famous, Honor Drummond turned and fled.

Exasperating female. She was driving him to Bedlam with her pretty little pleas and nonsensical speeches. Calling him a friend, indeed. It was like saying, "good boy" and then patting him on the head like she did her silly dog.

He looked at it, head low and tail uncharacteristically still as Lolly watched its mistress hurry to the house.

"Come here, boy," he called, setting down his brush as Lolly padded up to him. "Never fear," he said comfortingly as he leaned down to stroke the animal's back. "I doubt she's satisfied with the havoc she wreaked in my life. She will return to do more."

Disconcerting, how much he wished those words were true.

From their position at the parlor window, the Pithnevel girls saw Honor emerge from the stables. "I wonder what she had to say to Geoffrey," Iris mused aloud.

"Whatever it was," Hermione answered darkly, fingering the Pithnevel Pearls at her throat, "I think we had best redouble our efforts to keep them apart."

∾17∾

Stepping down from his carriage, Geoff straightened his cravat, then his cuffs, his waistcoat—anything to delay the moment he must go in to what must be the epitome of an awful Season. Some people are born to entertain, while some should never make the attempt, and the Throckmorton's, Geoff firmly believed, headed the latter category.

This ball would be a crashing bore, but why should that matter? His entire life had been deuced uneventful of late. He had not sipped a drink nor laid down a wager in days, and he could not remember the last time he'd frequented one of his clubs.

Oddly enough, it was not lack of opportunity that kept him from such pursuits. He'd had time aplenty on his hands. Indeed, it was quite daunting to realize how much Honor Drummond had filled up his days—especially now that she was no longer in them.

In light of that suspicious axle, he'd tried to stay near her. He'd made several attempts to engage her in various outings, but between his cousins, the baron, and the woman herself, Miss Drummond's time was so occupied, Geoff could never succeed.

This evening was a perfect example, he thought in exasperation as he forced himself to go inside. His uncle had asked him to escort Honor, yet when Geoff appeared in Pithnevel's foyer, well within the arranged time, he'd been informed that the baron had already seen to the task. Geoff had said splendid, he was just as happy to have the night to himself, but after a few hours of pacing, here he was, smiling inanely at Lady Throckmorton and wincing at the music emanating from the room below.

Courtesies done, he descended the stairs, determined to shake off this strange mood. True, the Throckmorton Ball was inevitably soporific, but he'd spent a lifetime circumventing ennui. Was he not a rake, a confirmed Dissolute, with a talent for finding diversion?

Scanning the room, he spotted Foxley and Bellington. Those two were always ready for a lark. Perhaps they could get up a game of cards, or talk Freddie Throckmorton into opening up his father's liquor drawer.

Yet Geoff made no move toward his friends. His eyes, he realized, had not quit their searching. He wanted . . . drat, he had no idea what he wanted, only that it did not involve betting and drinking the night away.

And then he saw Honor Drummond, on the far side of the room, and he forgot all about seeking diversion.

Standing beside the baron in unrelieved gray, she seemed like a shadow, all traces of the impish miss wiped away. She could be in mourning, Geoff thought. Lord knew she looked lifeless enough.

He told himself to feel angry, to wash his hands of the entire situation. The woman had made her proverbial bed and now she must get used to it. It was foolish to stand here watching her; there was nothing he could do.

"Geoff?" Startled, he looked at his sleeve. Attached to

it was a hand, which was likewise attached to Amanda Gratham. She, like her twin, peered at him with concern.

"I say, Geoff," Pandy said with a hint of exasperation. "Can you not hear? We've been chattering in your ear for this past age or two."

"I've always done my best to ignore you," he teased, trying to focus on the pair, though his gaze kept sliding back to Honor Drummond. "I have this vain hope that it will induce you to go away."

Following his gaze, they looked at each other. "Is it true?" Amanda asked in a considerably lowered tone. "Did someone truly try to hurt Miss Drummond?"

"Where did you . . . ?" He shook his head, annoyed to have been caught off guard. He must admit nothing; it would not do at all to set this pair along that track. "What utter nonsense," he bluffed. "I thought you knew better than to pay heed to rumor."

"Don't try to fob us off," Pandy said. "We happen to know it's no rumor."

"You should not believe everything you are told."

"No one ever tells us a thing." With a pout, Pandy nodded to where Lady Sarah was holding court. "We had to eavesdrop."

As Geoff frowned, Amanda tightened her grip on his sleeve. "You must do something, Geoff. We cannot like to think of Miss Drummond in danger."

"What can you expect me to do?" he asked irritably. "The baron has set himself up as watchdog. I can't get near the woman."

Amanda's eyes filled with a ready sympathy, but Pandy's radiated a speculative gleam. "I daresay we could get near her."

As the twins exchanged glances, a slow smile spread over both faces. Uncanny, how they communicated without words. And calamity was what that communication inevitably spelled for others.

"Now wait . . ." he started to say, but the pair flitted off and Geoff had no real desire to call them back. They would only ignore him in any case.

So he let his attention slide back to Honor, still holding that same rigid pose beside her baron, though she must be finding it increasingly difficult. Furrows had formed on her forehead, deepening as the minutes wore on, a sure sign that the concentration was taking its toll.

Hearing the orchestra strike up again, Geoff thought of their single dance, how her face had glowed as she frolicked around him. Could she resist the temptation were he to ask her to dance again?

Once, he would have tempted Miss Drummond for the sole purpose of leading her into trouble, but tonight, oddly enough, he wished only to set her free. He needed to see the real Honor, twirling and bouncing about on the dance floor with those green eyes alight with mischief. That was where she belonged, not posing there like some captive slave beside the unappreciative baron.

As if she could hear his thoughts, she looked up suddenly, her gaze linking with his. Jolted to his toes, Geoff took an unconscious step forward. Almost imperceptibly, she shook her head, as if to warn him away.

Yet the message in her eyes spoke otherwise. It pulled at him, that look, and he found himself taking another step.

Couples moved onto the dance floor, coming between them, and the link was snapped. Geoff muttered a low oath, and then another as he again found Honor in the crowd, this time trotting obediently behind the baron to form a set.

His sudden anger disturbed him. He told himself not to be so nonsensical, to be relieved that Honor was dancing with someone else. He should look at it as a narrow escape, not as if his pocket had just been picked. Jealousy implied a certain sense of ownership, after all, and nothing could be further from the truth.

Besides, it was merely a parody of dancing that she now performed. She went through the motions, as devoid of spirit as if this were some chore, and Geoff could find no evidence of the carefree pleasure she'd previously shown.

Watching, he felt his resentment build. If no one stopped this, the baron could break her completely. Or, considering her expressionless features as she left the dance floor, was it already too late?

I've got to talk to her, he decided, his feet moving forward before his brain could finish the thought.

But another tune had begun and he was forced to make his way around the outskirts of the dancing couples. His view of Honor was often blocked, yet her stance never altered. I will put a stop to this, he vowed. I will have her laughing in no time at all.

To his surprise, the Gratham twins got there before him. Fearing the worst—one could never predict what the pair might do next—Geoff paused to watch them. If they managed to spirit Honor away, he meant to follow.

But it was von Studhoff they took away, in the direction of Lady Sarah. Grinning, Geoff wondered if they had done so for him. He hurried his pace, determined to seize the opportunity, whatever the cause, or cost.

But showing the first sign of life in days, Honor glanced swiftly at the baron's back and darted out into the hall.

Geoff went after her. When she moved out onto the veranda, he slowed his pace, loathe to call attention to himself. It suddenly seemed wrong to disturb her stolen moment. Drinking in each breath of air, raising her face to be bathed by moonlight, she clearly savored the unexpected freedom. For Geoff, in that moment, it was quite enough just to watch her.

Gliding to the edge of the veranda, she took hold of the iron railing as she gazed up into the sky. She sighed, and the sound slammed into his chest. How weary she sounded. How lost.

He feared he must have echoed her sigh, for she whirled around to face him. "Oh, heavens, my lord Lennox, you startled me."

He stepped forward slowly—it would have been rude not to—and tried to keep his tone casual. "After all this time, can you not call me Geoff? You did say we were friends, did you not?"

She smiled. Her entire face seemed to radiate with it. "I hope so. But then, you really should call me Honor."

Gazing down at her, drinking in each tiny detail, he could feel an imaginary clock ticking away in his head. Absurd, to waste time chatting, to wallow in such elation merely because of a smile.

The smile faltered, then fell. "We should not be here together," she said, looking away. "The baron . . ."

She trailed off, but then, there was no need to say more. She had already conjured up the specter of her upcoming wedding, setting it loose to hover between them.

"Hang the baron!"

She tilted her head to look at him, as if wondering what had brought on such a remarkable outburst, while on his part Geoff was wondering much the same.

"But I cannot think the baron would want—"

"I said, hang the baron," he repeated with more feeling. "What about what *you* want?"

"What I want doesn't matter," she told him heatedly, blushing as she again looked away.

Geoff felt a bit heated himself. He reached out for her arm, forcing her to look at him. "Do you think I have no eyes? That I am so blind I cannot see that you despise him? Are you that stubborn, that rattle-headed and unimaginative, that you would cling to a man who makes you miserable?"

"Rattle-headed?" Her eyes were like daggers, but it was the strain in her voice that cut into him. "Unimaginative? On the contrary, I dream all the time. Each night, I picture a handsome prince, sweeping me up and out of this nightmare. Not just any prince, but one who cares more about me than what others might think of my misadventures. The sort of man who would not think twice about going down on his knee in a public place and telling the world he adores me."

"And yet you will settle for the baron?"

"There's a great deal of difference between dreams and real life." She shook off his hand and Geoff watched the fight go out of her, heard the passion fade from her voice. "There is no dashing prince, I've learned, nor anyone willing to dirty a knee on my behalf."

Geoff stared down at her, feeling helpless. In the face of such a confession, what could he possibly do?

At her startled expression, he realized that once more his body had reacted before his brain. Cradling her head with one hand as his other supported her back, he had every intention of kissing her thoroughly.

Not that it was a one-sided affair—far from it. Moaning softly, with not even a token resistance, her hands flew up to encircle his neck. He lost whatever control he might have maintained as her lips parted in welcome.

The gentle pressure he had first intended became a deep, hungry searching as he plunged into her mouth. He did not know what he sought, nor was he fully aware of what he'd found; he knew only that he had never felt quite so powerful, so aroused, or so incredibly complete.

Indeed, he would have happily gone on kissing her for-

ever, had there not been a none-too-discreet coughing off
to the right.

Even then, he would have ignored it; it was Honor who
broke away as if burned. Her eyes seemed impossibly
wide as she turned to face the intruder.

"Oh, Baron von Studhoff. I ... we ... I did not see
you."

"So it would seem." Arms folded across his chest, von
Studhoff eyed her coldly.

"His lordship was pointing out the stars," she said
quickly, regaining both wits and poise. "I insisted that
group of stars is Orion but he assures me it's Ursa Minor."

Geoff, recovering far more slowly, could only hope the
baron didn't quiz him. Even with his wits intact, he
wouldn't know Orion—or any other constellation—from a
hole in the ground.

But the stars appeared to be the last thing on the baron's
mind. "It was kind of Lennox to entertain you," he said
curtly to Honor, "but it is time for us to go."

"On the contrary, she was entertaining me." Impul-
sively, protectively, Geoff stepped forward, prepared to
suffer a hundred questions if the baron would thus leave
Honor alone. "She has quite a grasp on, er, astronomy. I
daresay one of the general's aides must have taught her
that, too."

Honor went stiff, like a doe scenting danger, and her
eyes held that sad, silent appeal. You can't retreat now,
Geoff thought desperately, but she was already withdraw-
ing.

With a wide smile, the baron extended a hand to her.
"Come, I promised Pithnevel I'd have you home early this
evening. You'll need your rest, my darling. Only three
more days until Sunday."

Outwardly, von Studhoff was every inch the eager, devoted bridegroom, yet as Honor placed her tiny hand in

his, something unpleasant wriggled along Geoff's spine. Watching her turn and walk off with the man, he could not stop himself from calling out, "Honor?"

She turned back momentarily. "It was a most unusual lesson, *Lord* Lennox," she said stiffly, "but I am afraid we cannot continue. It truly is time for me to go."

I've been dismissed, Geoff thought, and he had no choice but to watch her go. Boiling with helpless anger, he could not know who enraged him most; the baron, Miss Drummond, or more likely, himself.

He should never have kissed her. He felt a proper cad, not to mention a fool, and only a hopeless romantic could hope it would change a thing.

Three more days. The words pealed through his brain like a death knell.

Honor endured the carriage ride home, poised on the edge of her seat in anticipation of the baron's explosion. He had to have seen them, or at the very least, seen through her contrived excuse. Not even the dark could disguise how desperately she'd clung to the sweet perfection of that kiss.

But the baron said nothing. He talked on about wedding arrangements, their trip to his homeland, everything but what consumed Honor most. Part of her almost wished he would confront her, to have it out in the open. This way, she was left wondering if the moment had actually happened, or if she had merely dreamed it instead. The baron's silence was deliberate, she thought irrationally, as if he meant to take this precious memory away from her, too.

But deep down, she knew she should be glad he chose to overlook her indiscretion. Had she forgotten how desperately her father needed this wedding? For her, the moment had been sheer bliss, but she could not hope Lennox would attach much importance to it. He must have kissed a dozen starstruck girls and he would no doubt kiss a good dozen more.

Geoff, she thought softly, her mind caressing the name.

"We are here," the baron pronounced beside her. "Shall I escort you to the door?"

"There is no need," she said quickly, turning to let the footman help her down. "You too will want your rest."

He reached for her hand, letting his lips linger on her glove. It took all her will not to yank it back.

As if he knew this—and was amused by it—he took his time in letting her go. "Enjoy your sleep, my love," he taunted as she stepped down, "for I shall be keeping you quite busy in three days time."

Honor ran to the door, hearing his laughter behind her as his gaudy black carriage rattled away. Shuddering, she touched her lips, wanting to cry. Dear God, but after kissing Lennox, how could she ever again bear to be touched by the baron?

Oh, where was the prince, to sweep her out of this nightmare?

~18~

Arms folded as he leaned against the door, Geoff listened for the sound of a carriage. He had sent the butler to bed, convincing Hanson that everyone else had turned in, fully intending to guard the door in his stead.

And so he waited like an outraged parent. Von Studhoff had bustled her off, saying they must get home, yet Geoff had been waiting here for the better part of an hour. Where the devil were they? What on earth could have happened?

When he finally heard the carriage, he felt such over-whelming relief, he nearly rushed outside. In time, he recovered himself, knowing his uncle would not relish his brawling in the street. He would wait for von Studhoff to come to the door and then Geoff would confront him.

Grasping the knob, he realized he hadn't the least idea what he meant to say. In some hazy part of his mind, he supposed he planned to bring up the kiss, to ask why the man had so studiously ignored it. He needed to know how von Studhoff could show no reaction when Miss Drum-mond so clearly had. Any woman who could kiss him like that, Geoff wanted to point out, had no business marrying the baron.

But as he listened for footsteps, he realized there was but one set, light and graceful. Smiling grimly, he thought, good, he had quite a few questions for Honor as well.

She was tearing off her gloves as he opened the door, peeling them away as if they were diseased. "Thank you, Hanson," she muttered as she marched past, holding the offending items in front of her.

"Where have you been?"

She spun around, gloves dropping to the floor as she saw him. A faint blush crept into her cheeks. "At the ball. With the baron."

Geoff closed the door behind him and leaned back against it, his eyes never leaving her face. "All this time?"

"Throckmorton cornered us, made us inspect his stuffed head collection." She drew herself up, no doubt realizing he had no right to interrogate her. "If you don't mind, I have spent the night yawning and I would like to retire."

"Before we finish our conversation? You never did tell me why you mean to marry that lout."

The blush deepened, went beet red. "As I recall, we were not precisely conversing."

She seemed so stiff, so disapproving. He wished she would look at him, but she became suddenly intent upon retrieving her gloves. Aching to touch her, to feel her again in his arms, he moved closer. "Just so," he said softly. "And that's precisely what I wish to talk about."

"It would be best," she snapped, jamming the gloves into a ball between her fists, "if we just overlook the incident."

"Overlook it?" Geoff had never been slapped, but he imagined this was how it must feel. "Oh, I see. Forgetting one's impending nuptials while being swept away by passion simply is not good ton?"

"I was distraught." The glove ball was almost invisible. "Else it would never have happened."

Geoff could not remember ever feeling so angry, or so much the fool. What had he expected? That she'd say "the devil with convention" and fall again into his arms? "I beg your forgiveness then, for being such an inexcusable boor."

"No!" She shook her head, still refusing to face him. "You were . . . it was . . . wonderful. But don't you see? It doesn't change things at all. I must marry the baron."

He closed the distance between them, fingers itching for the feel of her. "Why?" he pressed. "You can't love him."

"Love is a luxury, my lord. One I can ill afford at the moment. I must concern myself more with practicality, with family loyalty and filial duty—"

"A pretty speech. So noble of you to think of your father's needs, but what of your own? You can't expect me to believe you look forward to a life with that pompous prig."

"I do." She tilted her chin defiantly.

She might sound resolute, but standing before her, gazing into her expressive eyes, Geoff could see the doubt and desperation. He reached for her, wanting nothing more than to hold her close to his heart, but she edged backward, her eyes wide and frightened. "I have made my choice," she said, her voice quavering, "and I will stay with it."

"Your choice?" he barked, moving closer. "Or was it your father's?"

"Leave off. You know nothing."

"Then pray, enlighten me." She turned to flee up the stairs, but he grabbed her wrist. "I need to know."

"What must you know?" she asked, blinking back tears. "That we are destitute? If someone does not soon pay his monstrous debt, the general will land in debtor's prison. I ask you, my lord, if it were your parent, what would you do?"

Stunned, Geoff released her wrist. Throughout, he had assumed it was the baron who wanted the general's money.

"I wished you had not asked," she said quietly. "I had not meant to burden you with this."

"Honoria?" Pithnevel called out from the top of the stairs. "Is that you?"

Honor looked at Geoff for a moment more, then with a quick, "I'm coming," turned to flee up the stairs.

Geoff watched her go, feeling an odd little twist in his gut. He felt stunned, and quite humbled, by her confession. From the day he had first met Honor Drummond, he'd insisted upon seeing the worst in her, yet at every turn, she had somehow proven him wrong.

He began to consider—truly consider—the sickening prospect of her shackled to the baron.

Three days' time, he thought. As the twins would say, something must be done indeed.

Despite tossing and turning for hours, Geoff still had no idea what that something would be early the next morning. Lying in bed, mulling over the events of the past few weeks, it occurred to him that he had not been thinking clearly since the whole wretched affair began. For had he been, he'd have wondered long before now what a prig like von Studhoff would want with an imp like Honor Drummond. The way the man treated her, it couldn't be love.

Odd, the baron's behavior last night. He had to have seen them together, yet he'd made no move to call Geoff out. He'd seemed determined to "overlook the incident," as if he took his cue from Honor.

Or was something a bit more sinister involved?

Sinister? Sitting up, Geoff wondered what made him

think of such a word. It must be this business with the broken axle. Making him see demons at every turn.

Setting his feet on the floor, he heard a carriage rattle into the stable below. A glance at his clock proved it was barely seven. Who on earth would be visiting at this ungodly hour of the morning?

Curious, he opened his door in time to hear Frampton speak to the groom downstairs. "Quick, shut the door. I do not want my rig seen from the street."

Then the man should take greater pains to be quiet, Geoff thought, for half of London could surely hear him.

One of which was Pithnevel, for he could now hear his uncle ask the groom to leave. Geoff, whose curiosity had nearly taken him down the stairs, eased the door shut to the merest crack. Better to remain unseen if he wished to learn what was afoot.

"Drummond is on his way back to London," Frampton said, his voice losing some of its volume, "and will soon be taking Honoria home with him. Is it not time we warned them both what von Studhoff is about?"

Any qualms Geoff might suffer over eavesdropping vanished at the mention of Honor's name.

"Unfortunately, the general plays an abysmal bluff," his uncle said. "He would give us away in an instant. No, I fear we must let the cards fall as they may."

This was no simple game of cards they discussed.

"I swear to you," Frampton insisted, "we can rely on the general's sense of honor to see us through."

"I hope so." Pithnevel's tone was somewhat doubtful. "Considering the size of his debt, one can almost understand the temptation to take the easy way out."

"Drummond won't sell government secrets, I tell you. He would as soon put a bullet in his skull."

Geoff felt the cold flash of apprehension. That was why

von Studhoff offered marriage? To use Honor to pry state secrets from her father?

"Let us hope it need not come to that," Pithnevel was saying. "As it is, I fear it is his daughter who shall suffer the most."

"Poor Honoria," Frampton said with a trace of sadness. "I still wish it had not been necessary to use her to set this trap. She will not have an easy time of it, if she does indeed marry the baron."

"It cannot be helped. Our duty, as you well know, is to think first of what will be best for the country we serve."

Geoff tightened his jaw. All well and good for England, but what about poor innocent Honor?

Andy had not known the half of it when she'd suggested the woman might need someone to look out for her.

Realizing there was no other candidate for the job, Geoff eased away from the door, going straight to his wardrobe. If his uncle and Frampton wished to play their war games, they would just have to find another pawn, for as of today, he was removing Miss Drummond from the field of play.

His first task, he decided as he threw on his clothing, would be to track down the general's man of business. He'd learn the names of the man's creditors and promptly pay them off. It might cause talk, but considering the circumstances, Geoff couldn't bring himself to care.

It was not until he went downstairs to order his curricle readied, and he saw Lord Frampton's rig, that he thought to wonder where the man and his uncle had gone.

No matter, he told himself with a shrug as he drove away. The important thing now was to keep Honor safe.

Pithnevel smiled as he watched his nephew speed off. "Well, he's gone."

"Do you think he heard?" Frampton asked, emerging from the hedges behind him.

"We must hope so." The smile faded, Pithnevel's features went grim. "A great deal depends on it."

Von Studhoff paced across the Drummond parlour in a fury of worry and anticipation. He checked his watch, angered further to find it past noon. After all his careful planning, must victory continue to elude him?

He could not wait to tell his French backers to go to the devil, for in a few days' time, he'd have adequate funds of his own. Once he supplied the correct information to the right ears, Napoleon would reward him with the land and the position he so richly deserved. The von Studhoff fortunes would be restored at last.

All he need do was get his hands on that information.

Where in creation was Drummond? Chafing with the delay, the baron paced furiously across the carpet. Even now, both armies could be marching toward Belgium. Before morning, he must know the enemy's strength.

Hearing the front door open, the baron paused to listen. At the low, cautious murmuring, he smiled. He could have told the butler it was too late to warn his master, that Drummond was already ensnared in a carefully designed trap.

"Von Studhoff?" Drummond asked as he burst into the room, clearly too weary to bother with the niceties. "What are you doing here at this hour?"

"It is time we had a chat, my friend," the baron told him with an ever-widening smile. "Time you explained precisely what you've been doing this past week or so."

Drummond stopped before him, his features wary. "I was on business, I told you."

"In Dover?" The baron quite enjoyed the man's spurt of alarm, that recognition of impending doom. "No, dear friend, my people have had you followed. We know exactly who your contacts were, and why they came to you. What we wish to know now, of course, is exactly what was said."

"I don't know what you can mean."

"Come now, don't play the fool. I want the number and location of your troops on the Continent, Herr Drummond. And the names of those who have been chosen to lead them."

"Impossible!" Drummond exploded, showing remarkable spirit for one in his position. "That is treason."

"On the contrary, think of it as survival. You won't last long in debtor's prison, you know. Nor, I think, will your daughter fare well in your absence."

"Honor has nothing to do with this."

Splendid, the way he rose to the bait. These English were nauseatingly self-sacrificing, but their Achilles' heel inevitably lay in their children. "I regret to inform you, but Honoria has everything to do with this. In two days' time, do not forget, she will become my wife."

"No."

"What do you propose, that she cry off?" Angered that the stubborn fool would not capitulate, von Studhoff forced himself to laugh. "Who then will pay your bills? No one else will have her now, you must realize. I have made certain of that."

"You have not touched her?" A small consolation, Drummond's look of horror.

"I had no need to." The baron chuckled. "A useful tool, your rumor mill, and so easy to manipulate. It doesn't seem to matter if the tales are true or not, though I must admit Honoria has done her best to lend them credence. She too is easily manipulated, I've found, and far too careless of her reputation. Rest assured, it is quite unlikely that anyone else will step in to pay off your debts."

"I can talk to my creditors. And Fairbright's a relative of sorts—he might offer a loan."

"Do you think so? But how humiliating for you, a mere soldier, admitting to the aristocratic Lady Sarah that you cannot manage your affairs. Will you tell her how many times I have had to come to your rescue? Your Lord Pithnevel is bound to wonder what you did to earn all that cash."

"Those were gifts, you said."

"Did I? Unfortunately, I shall not be here to be questioned. For you, it's either prison or the gallows, but for Honor . . ." he paused, smiling sympathetically, "I doubt life shall be easy for the child of a convicted spy."

The man began to sweat. "Do you mean to blackmail me?"

"I merely point out the facts, and the sad truth, Herr Drummond, is that I have you exactly where I want you. You truly must do as I say."

The man stood as stiff as a starched shirt point. "All along, Honor was right about you. I should have listened to her, but I kept counting the shillings, not the cost."

"And as you English say, it is now time to pay the piper. Will you give me my information, or shall your child pay the price?"

"I-I do not have it with me. I left my papers at the War Office, for my interview this afternoon with Pithnevel. Unless you wish to draw unnecessary suspicion, the earliest I can have that intelligence will be later on tonight."

Was he lying, stalling for time? Hard to believe—the general could not bluff his way out of a bowl of soup.

Still, von Studhoff had other means to enforce the man's obedience; it might be wise to employ them. "Very well, Herr Drummond," he said pleasantly. "I will return at midnight. I trust you will have the good sense to be waiting for me?"

"You leave me little choice."

"I am glad we understand each other." The baron smiled and went to the door. "Do not fear, my friend. I plan to make Honoria very, very happy. Provided, of course, that you continue to do as you're told."

Waiting to ask the general when they could expect Betsy to return from her visit to the country, Honor heard most of this conversation. Appalled, she barely managed to duck into the salon as the baron came into the hall. Indeed, she was still shaking when he went out the door. That awful, dreadful man. How dare he threaten her father!

She marched to the parlor, determined to assure the general that she did not fear being destitute, or ostracized, or any other awful state of affairs that man might cause, but she halted in the doorway, thoroughly nonplussed. Her poor, proud father sat slumped on a chair, his head hung in his hands. Part of her longed to rush to his side, but a more sensible part understood that it would kill him to have his daughter witness his moment of absolute shame.

Gulping painfully, she backed away. Von Studhoff was right; the general would rather die than have anyone see how low he had fallen. She could not turn to Lady Sarah, or Richard, or God forbid, Lennox. Had there been any hope in that quarter, Geoff would have spoken up last night.

No, she was quite on her own in this, she thought as she went up the stairs. She alone must dream up some way to stop the baron's threats.

The best solution, of course, would be for the general to confide the truth in Pithnevel, but her father seemed bent on protecting her. Such concern touched her deeply, but she knew it would be best for all concerned if she were not around to cause him worry.

Pausing at the top step, she felt hope flare in her heart. If she were to run off to ...

To where? she thought, stopping herself at once. In truth, she hadn't the funds or resources to ever break free of the baron.

Letting herself in her room, she tried not to panic. There must be some way out of this.

Two days, she thought desperately as she flopped face first on her bed. If she hoped to escape, she was swiftly running out of time.

$\sim$*19*$\sim$

Geoff strode into Pithnevel House, determined to talk to
Honor. After a frustrating morning tracking down Drummond's man of business, he'd suffered the most unsettling
news.

Staggering, the amount the general owed.

Still, Geoff would have paid all if he'd had the chance,
but an afternoon of relentless searching revealed that the
general's debts had been consolidated under one creditor—
the baron August von Studhoff himself.

Geoff saw no sense in approaching the man directly,
having quickly foreseen that von Studhoff would not allow
him to ease the vise with which he now held the Drummonds. The baron was like a great hairy spider, and poor
innocent Honor must be warned before she became
trapped within his web.

"Geoff?" His uncle stood at his study door. "Have you
a moment? I would speak to you."

"I need to see Miss Drummond."

"She is no longer here. The general came to take her
home some time ago."

Geoff muttered a few expletives under his breath.

His uncle smiled indulgently. "Actually, it was about Miss Drummond I wished to speak. Lady Sarah mentioned a broken axle?"

Geoff let loose a few more choice words. Confound the dowager's loose lips; he had not wanted his uncle drawn into this. Seeing no help for it, Geoff let himself be ushered into the study, but he refused to sit in the interrogation chair. "The wheelwright found nothing conclusive," he said testily from his position by the door. "Anything you might have been told is mere conjecture on Richard's part."

Pithnevel moved to stand behind his desk. "Indeed?"

Between a lack of sleep and the frustration of the day, Geoff had little patience. "Where is this leading?"

"I understand Miss Drummond was driving at the time."

Geoff felt that nasty pang in the pit of his stomach. "Perhaps, but what of it?"

Pithnevel sighed. "I had asked you to look after her. It would not seem you have been doing a proper job."

The gall of the man, Geoff thought, his hackles rising. If Honor needed protection, perhaps it was from men like Pithnevel himself. "I have done my best, under the circumstances," he all but growled.

"Then why does she keep landing in so many scrapes?"

"What would you have me do, use physical force? Throw her over my shoulder and drag her off?"

His uncle raised a brow but did not say a word. Geoff, fuming inside, began to picture himself sweeping up Honor and taking her away. . . .

As if she still stood before him, he could see her on the veranda, telling him about her dream.

His mind began to race, playing out the scene. If he acted the dashing prince, would she allow him to spirit her to safety? It would be one sure way to keep her from danger.

Yet if he did this, a tiny voice warned, he must be prepared to pay the price.

Still, what in truth was his choice? As Uncle Jack would maintain, a gentleman could not run from a damsel in distress, no matter what coil she placed him in. Geoff must prevent this marriage to the baron, even if it meant becoming embroiled in one himself.

Marriage, he thought, surprised at how little he hated the idea. Indeed, he was so caught up in his plans, he turned and left the study, completely unaware that his uncle still stood watching behind him.

Pithnevel chuckled softly. That took care of the daughter quite nicely. Now he must wait for the father to pay a visit.

Hermione placed a finger on her lips, cautioning her sister to quiet. Iris could be such a goose. This was no time to erupt into the giggles, merely because General Drummond appeared at their doorstep looking as if he had sipped one brandy too many at four in the afternoon. If they wished to learn what had brought him here in so frazzled a condition, they must remain as quiet as mice.

Motioning for Iris to stand guard, Hermione bent down to place an ear to the keyhole. To her chagrin, the blatantly agitated Drummond was muttering and proved difficult to hear. She caught only "the baron" and a very alarming "cry off" before Iris harrumphed behind her.

Hermione almost wept with frustration at the sound of footsteps rapidly approaching down the stairs. No sooner had she straightened than their cousin Geoffrey swept through the foyer on his way out the front door.

In his haste, a folded paper flew out of his hand. He bent down to retrieve it, then rose with the page clutched firmly in his grasp. Hermione, instantly curious, forgot the interview behind her and drifted closer. "Such hurry, cousin dear?" she called out. "Where is it you are going?"

"To stop a marriage," he tossed over his shoulder before slamming the door shut behind him.

In her mind, Hermione again heard the general mutter von Studhoff's name. Cry off? Drat that Geoffrey—he was not going to get her pearls.

"Iris," she cried, her voice ringing with determination. "Quick, fetch your bonnet. It is vital we go this instant and pay Miss Drummond a call."

Von Studhoff nearly jumped to the ceiling at the sound of the butler's forced cough. "May I help you, sir?" Rawlings asked with the blandest expression his features would allow. Difficult to tell what the butler was thinking; impossible to learn if he'd seen von Studhoff at the letter tray.

"I came to see Miss Drummond," the baron lied, wanting no one to guess he had authored that note. By the time the truth was known, it must be far too late. "I wished my visit to be a surprise, but I have since decided against disturbing her. After all, there shall be ample opportunity for us to talk in two days' time."

He could not like the pucker on Rawlings's brow. But then, there would soon be no need to tolerate his insolence. The butler was about to learn how short-lived his days of service would be.

"My earlier instructions were that she must not be annoyed by visitors," von Studhoff added, meaning to put this mere servant in his place. "I trust you have followed them?"

Something flickered in the man's eyes, but Rawlings said no, Miss Drummond had seen no one.

"Good. See that she is not disturbed for the rest of the day."

Rawlings seemed about to speak, but the baron firmly repeated, "No visitors!" in a tone that brooked no argument. The devil could take the butler, and his master, as well. Indeed, the baron thought with satisfaction as he risked a last swift glance at the letter tray. Come tomorrow, the general would know better than to go running to Pithnevel, and his insolent butler would be out on the streets.

Rawlings could barely conceal his distaste as he showed the baron out, and it was all he could do not to slam the door in his face. Having served the general these twelve years or more, he could not fathom how his master could want such an arrogant lout for his daughter.

The earl of Lennox, however, now there was a gentleman. Lennox did not barge into another's home and start barking orders. No, he politely asked Rawlings to deliver a letter, and then neatly, discreetly, tucked a few notes in his palm.

The earl's letter! Rawlings had meant to put it in the tray, but between this and that, he had been distracted. Removing it from an inside pocket now, he was about to set it down when he noticed there was already a letter in the tray.

Odd, but he couldn't remember it being delivered. As he lifted it up, he noticed the marked resemblance. Shifting each from hand to hand, he wondered if the baron had brought the other. Thinking back, the man had acted curiously. Guilty, almost. Oh, how very much Rawlings wished he could read what was inside the baron's note.

Curiosity nearly overwhelmed him, but years of proper training held the upper hand. Too, the letters were so identical, he was no longer certain which was from whom. Spying on the baron was one thing, but the earl was Quality, and Rawlings could never bring himself to treat Lennox—however inadvertently—in so scurvy a fashion.

The doorbell gonged behind him. Called to duty, he tossed both missives into the tray. In his haste to answer the summons, however, he did not see that one of the letters floated off the table and onto the floor.

The Pithnevel carriage pulled in just as the baron's black vehicle drove out of the square. Hermione smiled with pleasure, for all must be well if the baron had called on Miss Drummond. Yet when she raised a hand in salute, the baron, like Geoffrey, stared straight ahead. He seemed preoccupied and not apt to notice a thing.

Had he already been spurned? she thought in a panic. The instant their carriage stopped, she snapped at Iris to alight. They must not waste a moment if they hoped to repair whatever damage their ramshackle cousin might have wrought.

"We wish to see Miss Drummond at once," she told the butler as he opened the door.

Rawlings looked past them into the square. Hermione, seeing only the baron's departing carriage, thought this strange, but the butler apparently found what he sought. Grinning, he bid them enter while he ascertained whether or not his mistress was at home.

On their way to the parlor, Hermione noticed the letter tray, as well as the folded piece of paper, so white and familiar, lying inside. "We have been looking for our cousin, the earl of Lennox," she said offhandedly to the butler. "I don't suppose he's stopped in for a visit?"

"He was here earlier," Rawlings told her. "But he did not stay."

The moment the butler left them, Hermione sunk her fingers into her sister's wrist. "Quick, before he returns, we must get that letter."

"Reading another's mail? Oh, Hermione, should we?"

"It's from Geoffrey, you goose. Do we stop whatever mischief he is about, or would you prefer to give over the Pithnevel Pearls?"

"Oh."

"Oh, indeed." Yanking Iris by her arm, Hermione once more instructed her sister to stand guard while she grabbed the letter. Looking twice in all directions, her heart thumping painfully, Hermione had just snatched the note and read the first two lines when the doorbell gonged behind her.

She jumped a good two inches, and Iris let out a squeak. The letter slipped from her ice-cold fingers and went sailing between them to the floor. Diving simultaneously, she and Iris each reached for it, managed to rip the note in half.

The paper tore again when Hermione tried to wrest the other segment from Iris's grasp. Annoyed, and more panicked by the moment, she shoved her sister into the parlor, barely clearing the door as the butler descended the stairs.

Hearing the Gratham twins greet him, she and Iris eyed each other with dismay. They could not like the twins, not with the attention Lords Foxley and Bellington paid them, and Hermione felt the pair was too chummy with Geoffrey by half. It would be most unpleasant, were she and Iris caught pilfering their cousin's note.

Nor could Hermione chance it ever reaching Honor's hands. She had not thought Geoffrey had it in him to be so romantic, but the two lines she'd scanned had spoken of enduring love and profound devotion. The rest, she'd little doubt, would be enough to turn the most sensible head.

"Quick," she hissed at her sister, ripping like mad. "Tear your part to pieces and we'll hide it in this chair."

Hermione could hear approaching footsteps as she

jammed the shredded letter beneath the cushion. Standing up, she found Amanda Gratham at the door.

To her horror, she could see a few squares of white on the cushion, and one or two littering the floor. She sat quickly, hands scrambling behind her to remove the evidence, while her feet kicked the scraps under the chair.

Both twins gave her a funny look, but Iris, bless her, captured their attention by babbling on about their upcoming engagements, allotting no space for breath nor interruption, so that it was with visible relief that all four faces greeted the apologetic butler as he came into the room.

"Miss Drummond sends her regrets," he told them, "but she will not be able to visit with you this afternoon."

"Honor is ill?" Amanda asked. "I do hope it is nothing serious."

"Not at all. Mere fatigue. She would love to see you, but the baron order—er, suggested she rest this afternoon."

The baron still ruled the roost? Surely that was a good sign. Reassured, Hermione rose to her feet. She'd like to take the remains of that letter and piece it together to learn what her cousin meant to do, but at least Miss Drummond would not have it either. "No doubt Honoria wants to look her best for her wedding," she said, taking Pandora by the arm to lead her from the parlor. "And as her good friends, we shall of course see that her wishes are done."

"Of course." Pandora seemed bewildered but nonetheless she went with Hermione to follow the butler to the door.

In her anxiety to get home to watch her cousin, Hermione failed to notice that it took Amanda Gratham a good deal longer to leave the parlor.

Frowning, Honor watched out her bedroom window as the Pithnevels, then Grathams, drove away. She would have dearly loved to share a giggle with the twins, but how could she say yes to one set of visitors while telling the other no?

Besides, she was no fit company for anyone. She had paced this floor so often, it was a wonder any carpet remained beneath her feet. Minute after minute ticked by, and still she could find no solution. Short of some last moment miracle, she would be forced to marry the baron.

Her mind knew this, perhaps even accepted it, but her absurd heart refused to go along. She kept hoping, dreaming, so much so that when she heard footsteps in the hall, she let herself believe—if only for an instant—that it was her handsome prince, come to rescue her, after all.

Flinging open the door, she found only Rawlings. "Forgive me, miss. I had not meant to startle you, but I have come to ask about dinner. Since the general won't be dining in this evening, do you wish to be served downstairs, or would you prefer a tray in your room?"

"The general won't be here?"

"He gave the impression he would not be returning until late tonight."

Honor knew it was foolish to feel such disappointment. Had she actually hoped the general would defy von Studhoff? That they could talk, and together find some way out of this dilemma? She should know by now that her father would avoid her. She would only cry—they both knew it—and the general would rather face a thousand rampaging armies than a female's helpless tears.

"I don't suppose the general left a note?" she asked anyway. "Is there any message at all for me?"

"My heavens, I nearly forgot yet again. There were two letters, actually. Shall I get them for you?"

"No, no, I need the exercise." Shutting the door behind her, she fell into step beside Rawlings. "You said there were two letters? Are they both from the general?"

"Forgive me for lending that impression, miss, but in

truth, neither is from your father." He smiled tightly. "One came from the baron—at least I think he is responsible—while the other was delivered by the earl of Lennox."

Lennox? As Honor's heart did a little flip, her feet nearly missed a stair. "Lennox was here?" she asked, unable to keep the excitement out of her tone. "What did he say? What did he do?"

"He merely requested that you receive his letter. I asked if he expected an answer, but he said we could leave that up to you. I set it here in the ... now that's peculiar. Where do you suppose it could have gone?"

Honor looked at the empty tray, sharply disappointed. She could not know what Geoff had written, but she wanted that letter with all her heart. "It's got to be here," she said desperately. "Perhaps it blew off the tray." Getting down on her hands and knees, she searched along the floor.

"Here, miss, let me ..."

But she had already seen a telltale flash of white and with a relief that bordered on hysteria, she reached for it. "It's here. Oh, Rawlings, I've found it." Clasping the page to her chest, she beamed at the butler before turning to race up the stairs.

In her room, she kicked the door shut behind her and ripped off the seal in a fever of anxiety. Her hands trembled as she began to read.

"My dear Miss Drummond,

"It has come to my attention that you might stand in need of aid. I do not wish to alarm you, but I have learned the baron is not at all the sort with whom you should entrust your life, nor can I be convinced that you shall ever find happiness with such a man.

"I have thought a great deal on this, and it strikes me that if you wish to prevent future misery, you are

somewhat short of options. I can see but one way that
it can be done.

"I am not very good at this sort of thing, for I have
not had much practice, but I suppose I am quite capable of acquiring a special license. And failing that, I
daresay I can find the road to Scotland. If you would
be willing to place yourself in my care, I will do my
utmost to see that you *and* your father do not suffer
at the baron's hands.

"I shall be waiting at the entrance to your square at
precisely eleven this evening. If you should decide to
risk the future at my side, please join me there and
tell no one what we mean to do. Please forgive the
havey-cavey nature of such an arrangement, but I
swear to you, secrecy is vital. If the baron were to
learn of our plans, it could go poorly for us all.

"I trust you shall make the right decision.

> Until tonight,
> Your prince,
> Geoff "

Honor's vision blurred when she came to his name.
Brushing away the tears, she felt suddenly like dancing.
Here at the eleventh hour, just as she'd been ready to
admit utter defeat, her miracle had indeed happened.
Lennox—no, Geoff—had asked her to run off to be mar-
ried.

At least, she thought he had. Frowning, she read the
letter again to make certain. It was not the most direct proposal, but he did speak of special licenses and taking the
road to Scotland, so what else could he mean?

How like him, she thought fondly as she let her fingers
trace his cramped scrawl. He could not risk being emo-
tional; he must keep even this note on a businesslike level.
No words of love, nor even affection, just that quickly

scribbled "your prince" at the bottom. Yet in and of itself, it was quite enough to take her breath away.

But what was she doing, mooning over a letter like a moonling? Eleven was barely a few hours away. Missing her abigail more than ever, she began to grab things to stuff into her bandbox.

She forgot, in the flurry of activity, how Rawlings had mentioned two letters, that the baron's had never been found.

"I stayed behind to learn why Hermione so zealously guarded that chair," Amanda explained to Lady Sarah. "It is not at all like her to fret about misplaced scraps of paper."

"We've pasted it together the best we can," said Pandora, presenting the letter.

"A few pieces are missing," added Amanda. "I could only risk staying in the parlor a few minutes."

Lady Sarah frowned at the page. Lennox, asking Honor to run off with him? It wasn't like him to be so precipitous. She'd like to think her matchmaking had driven him to such desperation, but she feared a good deal more simmered beneath the surface, things of which she'd not been apprised.

"The gist of it is," Amanda said slowly, her pretty eyes clouded with concern. "As much as we wish to see Honor nicely settled, P and I agree that this cannot possibly be Geoff's hand. Either someone is playing a nasty trick . . ."

"Or," her sister finished darkly, "something far more nefarious must be involved."

~20~

Geoff strode out of White's, frustrated that he had yet to locate Foxley or Bellington. If he could not soon find someone to watch over that confounded dog, he just might have to let Lolly tag along. And while he might have come to tolerate the animal, he could see little value in canine company on a wedding trip.

His wedding. Hurrying to his curricle, he shook his head at that bizarre thought. His bewilderment had less to do with the possibility that he soon could be married and more with the fact that he quite enjoyed the idea. He, who'd taken pride in being a rogue extraordinaire, was actually grinning at the prospect of spending the rest of his days with the impossible Honor Drummond.

"I say, Stone, out to drown your sorrows?"

Geoff stopped in his tracks, dismay stealing over him at the sight of Fortesque leaning against his curricle.

"S'pose I should buy you a drink to commiserate. Poor devil. By tomorrow, your life won't be the same."

Geoff stiffened. How the deuce had Fortesque learned of his plans? Eyeing him with distaste, Geoff realized the man was so far gone in his cups, he could have blabbed in the ear of every gossip in town. He strode forward, wanting nothing more than to land a facer on that despicably slack jaw.

Fortesque grinned like the village idiot as he reached up to stroke the horse beside him. "Most regrettable for you, old chap, but these grays will soon be mine."

Strange, but all Geoff felt was relief. Fortesque meant their ridiculous wager, not his plan to marry Honor. "You've miscounted the days," he told him while separating the man's hand from his horse. "You haven't won yet. Miss Drummond has two more days to change her mind."

"Fear not." The dolt flashed a more imbecilic grin. "You will find the bridegroom has altered the schedule."

"What is this?" Geoff reached for Fortesque's collar. "What is the fiend plotting now?"

The man paled. Pallor meant nothing—many a sot went white before swooning into alcoholic oblivion—but Fortesque seemed to sober before his eyes. "It-it's nothing, Stone. I-I was just bamming you."

Geoff could smell the alcohol on his breath; the fumes alone were enough to intoxicate him. Fortesque had been drinking and gaming a great deal of late, he realized, yet from where had he gotten the funds to maintain such a life-style? Who paid his bills? More to the point, why?

"You've been working for the baron!" Geoff accused, putting two and two together. "Did he pay you to tamper with my axle?"

"No, I swear—"

"Save the protestations. Just tell me why."

Geoff tightened his grasp on the collar, forcing the fool to his toes. Lolly, growling at the general area of the seat of his pants, helped loosen the man's tongue. "I swear, I know naught about any axle," a red-faced Fortesque croaked out. "I was merely paid to lead Miss Drummond to disgrace herself."

"Like urging her to sign her name in the betting book?" Geoff gave an extra tug on the collar. "Did it never occur to you that this would give von Studhoff an excuse to cry off? That you would thus stand to lose our wager?"

"No! He swore that he meant to marry Miss Drummond. He merely wished to make certain no one else would want her."

Clever man, the baron, cutting off all avenues of her escape. Geoff gave the collar an added squeeze, and lifted his captive a half inch off the ground. "And just what does he have planned for Miss Drummond tonight?"

"Nothing." Rising another half inch, Fortesque began to whine. "Have mercy, Stone, you know I can't tell you. The baron would kill me."

"And I shall kill you if you don't." As if in reinforcement, Lolly growled menacingly at his posterior.

"He's taking her to Portsmouth. Leave off, will you? I can't breathe."

"He means to abduct her?"

"Don't be absurd. He's just getting married."

"The last I recall, we had churches here in London."

"Of course we do, but the baron wants to spare Drummond the expense and worry of a public wedding."

"How considerate of him. But most men wish to be there to give their only child away."

"The baron's no ogre, Stone. In fact, I'm to go to the general later tonight to tell him the new plan. The baron wants Drummond to meet them in Portsmouth."

"I'll just bet he does." Fortesque might be stupid enough to swallow such pulp, but Geoff knew better. Drummond must have proved less manageable than the baron had hoped, and he now had to threaten Honor to change her father's mind. "Did the baron ask him to bring anything along?" Geoff asked, though he had little hope that Fortesque would know about the military information von Studhoff must seek.

"Nothing specific. I was told to tell Drummond he would know what was needed."

The man was too stupid to live, Geoff thought in disgust, but as much as he'd love to put Fortesque out of commission, he could not waste the time. Releasing his grip, he watched the man go staggering backward, tripping over Lolly and falling on his rear.

On another day, Geoff would have found this amusing, but his mind was racing ahead. "Don't think we are through," he flung over his shoulder as he climbed into his curricle, Lolly leaping up behind him. "If Miss Drummond should suffer so much as a sniffle, I shall be coming after you."

He did not bother to look back to see the effect of his threat. Slapping the reins, he knew only that he must get to Honor before it was too late.

There was an hour yet to go, but Honor waited in the shrubbery, her bandbox at her feet, prepared to move at a moment's notice. She was not about to give Lennox any reason to change his mind.

If he came at all. Glancing uneasily about, she wished the clouds would stop scurrying across the moon. Each new shadow seemed to reinforce her doubts. That letter could be a hoax. What would she do if Lennox never did come to her rescue?

When a vehicle entered the square, she all but danced for joy. "Thank you," she told Geoff silently as she gathered up her bandbox and rushed toward the closed carriage. In all the excitement, she decided, he must have forgotten they were to meet *outside* the square.

The coachman waited beside the vehicle, nearly jumping out of his livery as she stepped up behind him. He must have anticipated a more conventional exit through the front door.

His lordship would join them on the road, he informed her. If Miss Drummond would kindly step into the vehicle, he would escort her to him at once.

Feeling a sudden trepidation, Honor glanced back at her father's house. What she was about to do was so . . . so impulsive, and everything she had promised the general she would never again do.

Yet it was Geoff who waited for her; reluctantly gallant Geoff who'd so amazingly offered marriage.

There really was no choice. Sighing, she stepped into the carriage.

"What do you mean, she's not here?" Geoff stared at the butler, feeling a bit ill. "She has to be home. It's not yet eleven."

If Rawlings saw something odd in that statement, he was too well trained to show it. Or perhaps merely too worried. "I am sorry, my lord, but I'm not at liberty to—"

"Hang the propriety, Rawlings. If you know where Miss Drummond is, I need to be told at once. I have reason to believe the baron means to abduct her."

"Oh my. When I saw her rushing out with her bandbox, I thought she meant merely to run away again. I do not think she is happy about her upcoming marriage."

"None of us are."

Rawlings gave a tight smile. "Quite so. If I may be so bold as to mention this, the baron did act suspiciously earlier in the day. And then too, there was that carriage parked outside—"

"Carriage? When?"

"Barely ten minutes ago. You don't suppose . . ."

Geoff never answered him. Leaping back into his curricle with the ever-vigilant Lolly beside him, he turned his horses for Portsmouth.

Rattling along in the hired carriage, Honor tried to pull rein on her conflicting emotions. It seemed that with every bump in the road, her mind wished to change course.

For a mellow moment, she dreamed of what might happen when the carriage at last stopped. As the door opened, there would be a smiling Geoff, holding out his arms in welcome. She would fall into them, eager to be thoroughly kissed.

Yet even as she licked her lips in anticipation, the carriage hit another rut and her thoughts veered off on another track. Why hadn't Geoff himself come to fetch her? she wondered uneasily. Why, if he wished to protect her, would he leave her in the care of a servant she did not know?

Now, with time to truly think on it, perhaps this marriage proposal was a bit too good to be true. A man like Lennox could have his pick of women, so why would he choose an Honor Drummond?

By the time the carriage jerked to a halt, Honor had worked herself into a state of near panic. If she'd misread his intentions—or worse, if this proved to be some cruel joke—she would simply die of humiliation.

She did not intentionally hold her breath as the carriage door opened; her lungs merely refused to function. Until she could see Geoff's face, until she saw that beloved grin, she feared she might never breathe again.

She was wrong, of course, for the instant she saw the baron's features, the air rushed painfully into her lungs.

"You are late," he said, holding out a hand to pull her to the ground. "You were told to be ready by ten."

Stepping down, Honor might have argued that the letter had mentioned eleven, but she was too anxiously searching for Geoff. If the baron had harmed one hair on that beautiful auburn head . . .

"Looking for Lennox?" von Studhoff asked, his voice ominously low. "Don't waste your time. It wasn't he who summoned you. Forgive the ruse, my dear, but I knew no other way to make certain you would come."

"*You* wrote that letter?" Inside, Honor was beginning to feel sick. "I-I don't believe it."

"No? Is it easier to believe a rake would resort to marriage? Or heavens, that he'd choose a hoyden like you? How naive of you to set such refinement on a kiss."

She cringed. So he *had* seen them together. How like von Studhoff to save the accusation for when it would hurt her most. "But then," he added maliciously, "you cannot have known about his wager."

Honor felt her stomach drop. "Wager?"

"Lennox bet Fortesque his curricle and pair that he could put a stop to our wedding. He must have been feeling desperate indeed to resort to that kiss. How frustrating for him when I failed to make a scene."

So that was why Geoff had waited for her that night. When the baron had not cancelled their marriage, he'd hoped to convince her to cry off instead.

Feeling sicker by the moment, she realized just how foolishly she'd been dreaming. All she had ever meant to Lennox was winning that bet. There would be no gallant rescue. Von Studhoff's trap was good and tightly sprung.

As if seeing this himself, the baron smiled nastily. "What am I to do, my love? Learning my intended has run off to marry another man hardly bodes well for wedded bliss."

"No one is forcing you to marry me."

"No? But I now feel it my duty to teach you to be a proper wife."

"I may have played the gullible fool, but I am not so

naive as that. You only want to marry me to make certain my father gives you the information you need. You think abducting me will force him to give it over."

If surprised by her knowledge, he certainly didn't show it. He merely chuckled and gestured toward his carriage. "So glad you understand. Now let's get to Portsmouth and be done with it. I find I cannot wait to have a father-in-law in the War Office. Most convenient to have such a source of information beneath my thumb."

"You can't get away with this."

"On the contrary." Taking her by the arm, he nudged her toward the carriage. "Your father is at the War Office and won't learn of your disappearance until later tonight. Quite frankly, my dear, who else will even notice you are gone?"

"My father went to Pithnevel?" Honor felt a rush of pride. "I knew all along he would tell the truth."

The baron narrowed his gaze and a menacing note crept into his tone. "You'd best say a prayer he is retrieving the intelligence I seek and not speaking to Pithnevel." Leering down at her, he gave her arm a painful yank. "You cannot hope things will go well for you once your usefulness comes to an end."

"Wait!" Honor wrenched free of his grasp. "What is that? Do I hear a vehicle approaching?"

"That ruse has been overdone," the baron snapped, but then he frowned, suggesting that he too must have heard horses. "It's hardly an isolated thoroughfare," he added. "I daresay it's some drunk sot, careening his way home from town. Get in the carriage, while I wave him on his way."

With alarm, Honor noticed the baron now brandished a pistol. "Please, you won't shoot him?"

"Not him, you. If you do not get in that carriage, I shall see to it that you go limping down the aisle."

Seeing no help for it, Honor backed toward the carriage.

"Not that one," he barked. "We shall ride in my vehicle. Lawrence?" he shouted to the coachman. "Be ready to drive off a moment's notice."

But Honor had no time to cross the distance, for the "sot" was careening indeed. He traveled so fast that by the time he saw them and pulled on the reins, it was a good distance down the road before he could come to a halt.

With an oath, the baron stomped toward him, tucking the pistol back within his waistcoat. "Go on, there's no need to stop," he shouted to the newcomer, waving his hands. "Just changing vehicles. We are not stranded at all."

Staring after him, Honor realized this was her chance to escape. It would be rough going, crossing these isolated fields, but the baron was so involved with shooing off the stranger, it would be some time before he noticed she was no longer there.

Lifting up her skirts, she began to run.

~ 21 ~

Hermione grinned at her sister. It had been so daring of them, following their cousin to Drummond House and then racing back here to report Geoffrey's activities to their father. Daring, and so productive. Barely had they finished speaking when Papa was barking out orders to the servants and hopping into his carriage to tear down the street.

And that should put paid to whatever Geoffrey had been planning. Hooking an arm in her sister's, Hermione led Iris upstairs to choose their dresses for Sunday. They could take turns wearing the pearls when Miss Drummond wed the baron.

Honor had gone no more than three steps when she heard the telltale bark. If Lolly were here, then . . .

"Changing vehicles, von Studhoff? Isn't this trip a bit unexpected?"

As she recognized Geoff's voice, her knees went weak with relief. Even if he hadn't written that letter, the fact that he'd come to her rescue must mean something.

Von Studhoff stopped, as if to stand his ground. "My

trip is no more unexpected than your appearance here, Lennox," he all but snarled. "Does nothing stop you?"

"I take that to mean you did indeed tamper with my axle. Was it to frighten me off, or had you meant something a bit more drastic?"

"Were you not so persistent, I'd have no need to be drastic. But no, you must win your wager with Fortesque. Gambling will be the finish of you British yet."

Honor halted, the wind knocked from her sails. The bet. Of course, that was why Geoff had come.

"Simply give Miss Drummond over into my care, Baron, and you need not bother with us British again."

"She won't go with you." The baron's hand reached into his waistcoat. The gun, Honor thought in alarm, even as the baron chuckled and added, "Go on, ask her yourself."

Geoff stood not ten yards away, his arm reaching out for her, and it took all her will to resist the temptation. Even knowing his true motives, she still longed to go with him, to stand—however briefly—at his side.

But she could not let herself forget the pistol, hidden from view. "The baron is right," she said, afraid that if she so much as mentioned the gun, the man would use it.

"There is no further need to let him bully you. I plan to discharge your father's debts. Just come with me now—"

"No!" she bit out desperately. How could a man who kissed her so passionately be so determined to win a stupid bet? "No," she repeated desperately. "I am not going anywhere with you."

"Of all the . . ." Even as Geoff strode forward, the baron yanked out and aimed his weapon.

"Stop!" she cried, "he's got a—"

Before she could finish her warning, the gun went off. She felt the explosion as if it had ripped into her chest, but in truth, the bullet went straight for Geoff's skull. She watched in horror as he fell backward into the ditch.

Not satisfied, the baron reloaded. Honor rushed at him, knowing she could not possibly move fast enough. Dear God, nothing would stop the fiend from killing Geoff.

But she'd forgotten the dog. Jumping for von Studhoff's throat, Lolly deflected his aim, causing the bullet to sail harmlessly past Honor and into the carriage door behind her. As the baron tried to shield himself, the pistol went flying.

Having hated the man for some time, Lolly took great pleasure in wrestling him to the ground. Honor reached for the gun, keeping it trained on the wriggling pair—as a precaution—while she edged back toward the ditch.

"Honor!" she heard her father cry out.

Thoroughly stunned, she turned to see him hop down from his phaeton. Pulling up behind was Pithnevel and a wagonload of soldiers. In all the excitement, she had failed to hear their approach.

The general rushed to her side. "My God, we heard gunfire. Are you all right?"

"It would seem your daughter has things well in hand," Pithnevel said, nodding at the weapon as he too alit. "With no little thanks to that dog."

Honor felt her arm go limp. Taking the pistol, her father gathered her close. "Thank God. If anything had happened to you, I'd never have forgiven myself."

He held her so tightly, she could scarcely breathe. *He does love me*, Honor thought in a daze.

"Child, had I known it would come to this—"

"You couldn't," Pithnevel broke in. "We all believed that if we gave the baron the incorrect information, it would suffice. None of us imagined he'd resort to abduction. It seems I did not anticipate all eventualities, after all."

"Geoff—" Honor began, trying to break free so she could go to him.

"Precisely," Pithnevel interrupted again. "I expected my nephew to take care of you, but as ever, Geoff seems to be off gallivanting somewhere else."

"But he—"

"That boy inevitably finds some way to disappoint me," Pithnevel went on, ignoring her attempts to point to the ditch. "If not for that dog . . . I say, will someone kindly remove the beast from the baron's throat? We do want the man able to speak at his trial."

"I know that dog," the general said, going suddenly stiff. "I say, isn't that . . ."

As he pulled away, Honor grabbed the opportunity to go to the ignored and much-maligned Geoff.

The ditch was not a deep one—nor was it filled, so she dropped at once, cradling his head in her lap to assess the damage. Though his temple bled profusely, she could see it had been a glancing blow, that he was more dazed than in any real danger of dying. "You silly man, is any wager worth this?" she asked, fighting off tears. "Why didn't you leave when you had the chance?"

His lids flickered open, though his eyes remained too glazed to focus. "There are three things from which a gentleman never runs," he told her groggily. "A sure bet, a damsel in distress, and whatever . . . whatever . . ."

He faded off, but there was no need for him to finish. Suddenly chilled, Honor whispered, ". . . whatever coil the first two land him in."

She had heard those words before—the night she'd run from Jeremy Wharton.

And now, she could understand the inconsistencies. All along, it had been more than just winning that bet; Geoff had meant to do to her what she had done to his good friend. Her public humiliation must have seemed the perfect revenge.

He had never cared about her at all.

"So he *is* here," Pithnevel said softly beside her.

"He's been wounded." Hard to believe that flat, matter-of-fact tone came from her lips, when inside she felt like dying. "Nothing serious, but he's bled a good deal."

"Captain?" Pithnevel called out. "Quickly, a litter. We have an injury here. Come," he added gently to Honor, urging her to her feet. "Let them take him to the surgeon. Poor Geoff, I seem to have underestimated him."

"He risked his life for me." Whatever his motives, this much was true. "You should be very proud of him."

"I am." Pithnevel watched her carefully. "Though he did not do this for me. But then, you must know this."

Honor turned away. She should leave before she blurted out what she *did* know. Now that Geoff had at last earned the respect he'd always sought from his uncle, why say anything to tarnish it? It would do nothing to ease her pain.

Looking down at him one last time, trying to memorize his features, she realized how very much she was going to miss Geoff. Wager or not, revenge or not, it had been a jolly good spree while it lasted.

Taking a deep breath, she forced herself to walk away. As the soldiers went by with the litter, she called out for them to be gentle, but her voice broke before she finished the words. It was as well, she told herself sternly, for she truly had no say at all in whatever might happen to him next.

Woodenly, she marched to her father's phaeton. Let them accuse her of stealing it again; what difference would it make? After tonight, the tongues would be wagging no matter what she chose to do.

Climbing into the vehicle, she realized she had been

right. Small satisfaction, but there truly were no princes for her, no one eager to dirty a knee in her behalf.

As she lifted up the reins, Lolly leaped onto the seat beside her. "Time to go home to Drummond Manor," she told her pet as she angrily brushed away the tears. "It would seem another disastrous Season has come to an end."

Feeling himself lifted in the air, Geoff came awake. Painfully, for his head throbbed like the very devil. In all, he would by far prefer to have stayed asleep.

Slowly, it all came rushing back—the mad chase, the baron—"Honor?"

"Do not fret, she's safe," his uncle said reassuringly beside him. "Be still, Geoff. As it is, I fear this litter will not hold you."

"Uncle Cyrus? How did you come to be here?"

"We're off to the surgeon to fix that nasty hole in your head. And I came because of your letter to Miss Drummond."

"You read my letter?" As groggy as he was, Geoff felt the cold jolt of embarrassment.

"What I could. It was quite torn up when the twins brought it to Lady Sarah, so we had difficulty ascertaining your exact destination."

The twins? Lady Sarah? Had his letter been bandied about half the town?

And what was this about it being torn? He hadn't agonized over every syllable, merely so Honor could rip it to bits. Deuce take it, had she meant to marry her dratted baron all along?

Pithnevel supervised Geoff's placement in his carriage, dismissing the soldiers when they were done. "It is quite fortunate Hermione learned you were off to Drummond House," he told Geoff when they were alone. "As it was, you were tooling off when we arrived. You led us a merry chase, my boy. I fear my horses will never be the same."

"Haste seemed vital. I thought Honor was in danger."

"So she was. I must say, you did admirably. Granted, eloping might have been a bit excessive, but the end result was quite to the point."

Even in his stupor, Geoff realized what his uncle was saying. "You *wanted* me to prevent her marriage to the baron? Good lord, why did you never come right out and say so?"

"Come now, we both know you've always done the exact opposite of what I request. This time, the stakes were far too high to risk failure. I had to keep Honoria safe."

The strategy didn't quite work, Geoff thought bitterly. "I let the baron get to her, anyway."

"It is not your fault she chose to go off with the man."

Geoff winced. "What of von Studhoff? Did he escape?"

"On the contrary. Thanks to you, I will now be taking him into custody to face charges of treason."

"And Honor?"

"Miss Drummond, actually, has gone off in her father's phaeton. The last I saw, the general was in pursuit, but whether he is chasing after his daughter, or that dog of hers, I cannot say. Do not fret about it—getting you well is the thing now. Captain?" he called out, stepping down from his carriage. "Take him to the surgeon at once, then meet me at the gaol."

As the carriage rolled away, Geoff shut his eyes. So Honor had run off once more, not even bothering to see how he fared. And worse, she'd taken the dog with her.

So much for playing her prince, he thought wearily. Like everyone else, she thought him better suited to the role of court jester.

Alone in the wagon, he fancied he could hear her words echo with each rattle of the wheels upon the road. "I am not going anywhere with you," she'd said, backing up the rejection by then running away.

So be it. Forcing his eyes open to stare at the star-filled sky, he told himself that it had been a momentary aberration, rushing out like some knight in armor, but he'd be pickled in potato juice before he'd compound such romantic nonsense by wallowing in useless regret.

He was actually relieved that it had come to this. No need to worry about what that woman would do next; at last, his life would be his own.

Once a rake, always a rake, his uncle Jack would have said. And just as soon as Geoff recovered from this wound, he meant to frequent each club, play every gaming table, and visit the home of each Fashionable Impure, until he quite forgot that this night—this month—had ever happened.

Confound it all, it was a good plan. He should be happy, ecstatic. Yet why, he asked the stars above, must he keep hearing that impossible woman's laugh and keep seeing only her smile?

There was no answer, of course. Only that incessant rattle of the wheels, as hollow and empty as the years stretching ahead.

❧ 22 ❧

Geoff could not help but admire the improvements to the place as he walked through the doors of Fairbright Manor. One day soon—after Richard's wedding trip—he must sit his friend down to ask his advice about dry rot and crumbling mortar. It would be nice to turn Lennox Hall into such a showplace.

Handing his hat to Richard's butler, Geoff marvelled at the pride he now felt in his estate. In his three-week recuperation there, he'd become so caught up in the details of management, not once had he thought of returning to the gaming tables or attending the various social affairs in London. Indeed, the bucolic tranquility was enough to start him thinking it just might be time for settling down.

Uneasily, he thought of the wedding ceremony this morning. Watching Richard and Andy exchange such loving glances as they traded vows, Geoff had felt that now familiar longing, and before he could stop himself, he'd been scanning the church for Honor Drummond.

It had annoyed him—nay, this constant need to find her frightened him—so badly, he had marched out of that church without looking back. Driving his grays over the fields of Richard's estate, he kept thinking of his letter, torn in so many pieces, and he'd had a sudden, horrifying vision of his heart in a similar state.

He'd come to the house to put in an appearance, feeling he owed that much to the newlywed pair, but he fully intended to go the instant he'd paid his respects. People at weddings were inevitably inane, and the last thing he wished was to be slapped on the back with an "Eh, old chap, aren't you next?"

"Geoff!" He'd barely cleared the ballroom doorway before the Gratham twins and their shadows, Foxley and Bellington, surrounded him. "Where have you been?" Amanda asked. "The ceremony's been over for hours."

"I drove around a bit. I found the air a bit stuffy— wanted to clear my head."

Everyone looked at the scar on his brow and then just as swiftly looked away. The one good thing about having such a wound was that even an oblique reference was apt to rapidly change the subject.

"Isn't this a frightful crush?" Pandora piped up, looking out over the crowded ballroom. "Half of London seems to be here."

"Now with Napoleon put to pasture," Adam said, "we're all out to celebrate."

Jamie grinned. "Save old Forty, who took off for parts unknown. No doubt trying to save face, after losing that wager. He was offering a ride in the park in Geoff's rig to the ladies when he heard the buzz about the baron's arrest."

Geoff thought it less likely the man was eluding embarrassment than keeping two steps ahead of Pithnevel. Even with matters resolved on the Continent, the War Office must have questions about how so much cash from that traitor, von Studhoff, found its way into the Fortesque accounts.

"You must be glad to have won that bet," Adam said, patting him on the back. "Must do your heart good to know your curricle and pair are safe."

Aware of the Pithnevel Pearls in his pocket, Geoff thought of the other bet he had won. Yet neither, in all truth, had been particularly good for his heart.

"Never mind his rig." Amanda gave Adam a frown. "What matters more is that Honor Drummond is safe."

Drat, must he react each time her name was mentioned?

"I haven't seen you two talking," Pandy added. "You must have missed her."

"I have not. If I've missed anyone it was the dog. I keep meaning to seek out the general to see just what became of him."

"A dog's an 'it,' not a 'he,' Geoff." Pandora gave him a strange look. "And I didn't mean *miss*, as in wish for her company. I meant, didn't you speak with her today?"

"Honor is here?"

"Why, yes. The biddies insisted she be excluded, since it was said she'd tried to run out on a second marriage—"

"—which is patently unfair," Amanda said vehemently. "She didn't and besides, anyone in their right mind would run away from a dreadful man like the baron."

Pandora smiled at her twin. "Which is precisely why Andy insists we put up a united front. We are all to speak to Honor, and you gentlemen must ask her to dance. By showing the others that Honor is our friend, everyone else will have no choice but to eventually accept her."

Jamie shook his head. "Andy's plan doesn't seem to be working. Her guests are snubbing Honor quite viciously. If you will notice, she's taken to hiding in the shadows."

No, Geoff thought desperately, looking everywhere but at the figure by the punch bowl. He was not about to be sucked into this again. "I really must pay my respects to Richard," he said, breaking away hastily. He might be a fool when it came to love, he told himself as he crossed the room, but he was not fool enough to risk that emotion twice.

"She's over there," a voice croaked behind him, and he felt the too-familiar poke of Lady Sarah's cane. "And having a miserable time of it, too."

"I can't know who you mean."

"Can't you?" Infuriatingly, she smiled at him, and nodded off to their right.

It was a mistake, looking to where she gestured, for the moment his eyes found Honor, Geoff knew he was lost. How defiantly she held up her chin, how stubbornly she refused to wilt under the rejection. Deuce take it, but just the mere sight of her had him wanting to go out tilting windmills in her behalf.

"Ah, yes, I'm glad you reminded me," he said stiffly, annoyed by this. "As I recall, you owe me a farthing. Since there will be no wedding, I won our wager."

Eyeing him speculatively, Lady Sarah reached into her reticule to extract a coin. "Never let it be said that I reneged on a bet. But tell me, have you even asked her yet?"

"I beg your pardon?"

"I must say, Lennox, I never thought you to be such a coward. You were brave enough in that business with von Studhoff."

"We both know I had little to do with that rescue. It was my uncle, with help from yourself, who manufactured it."

"Oh?" Lady Sarah pressed. "No one forced you to chase after the chit, and no one said you had to take a bullet in the head."

Geoff touched his scar. "Perhaps I knew ahead of time that the baron had atrocious aim."

Sarah snorted. "You faced up to that bully, yet now you balk at facing a chit half his size."

"If you refer to Miss Drummond, I can assure you I do not balk. I simply have nothing to say to the woman."

"You should talk to her. I myself learned a curious thing. Did you know she received *two* letters that day?"

Geoff refused to respond.

"Personally, I thought the missive we found far too flowery to come from your pen. You'd be more likely to make marriage sound like a business arrangement."

Geoff bristled. "Just because I am not romantical—"

She held up a hand. "The point is, the baron must have written the second letter, pretending to be you."

"But why the deuce do that?"

"Because he knew Honor would respond to you."

What an interesting concept.

"It's all academic, actually," Sarah continued. "Your cousin has confessed that she stole the baron's letter. Thinking it was from you, she tore it up. The first one, the one Honor responded to, had to come from you."

Dazed, Geoff tried to take it all in. Honor hadn't torn up his letter. She had read it—businesslike tone and all—and responded by packing her bags and coming out to meet him.

But the more he thought about it, the less sense her subsequent behavior made. "But all was resolved with the baron," he thought aloud. "Why did she then run away?"

"I really cannot say. You shall have to ask her that yourself."

Geoff let his gaze find, and then rest upon Honor. Confound it, he could at least talk to the woman. Show the crowd that he wasn't shunning her, put up a united front. Wasn't that what the twins said Andy wanted?

Yet talking was the furthest thing from his mind as he neared her. His gaze kept drifting toward her mouth; his body kept remembering their kiss.

As if sensing his approach, she turned suddenly, and for

a wonderful instant, her entire face glowed. Geoff had time enough to think, *She's happy to see me*, before she averted her gaze to the punch bowl.

"My Lord Lennox," she said with all the animation of a twig. "How nice to see you looking so well."

"Honor, I—"

"It is kind of you to come over, but there is no real need. Andy means well, pestering you all to make the effort, but truly, I am just fine. I am having the time of my life."

"Guarding the punch bowl?"

She winced, but whatever her other faults, she was not one to fold at first blow. "The punch is quite good," she pressed on. "If you'd like, I could pour you a cup."

"No, thank you. Actually, I wanted to ask—"

"About Lolly? He's fine, I assure you, though he misses you dreadfully." She hurried over the words, as if intent upon preventing anything Geoff might say. "The general has quite changed his thinking about him. Now that the baron is in prison, and the debt need no longer be paid, the general is a new man. He insists Lolly must be treated like a hero, for having saved my life, and claims he won't even mind if Aphrodite's litter has pronounced golden brown markings. He is just that happy to have his daughter safe and well."

She drew in a deep breath, as if to inflate her courage, though with all that quick talking, she clearly had need of air. "I've told the general Lolly was not the only hero that night. Coming to my rescue like that . . . well, I want you to know how overwhelmingly grateful I shall always be."

"You chose a strange way to show it. Running off, with nary a word."

She went to the bowl and began ladling punch into a cup. "I assumed you'd prefer it that way. I remembered, you see, when you spoke of the three things a gentleman never runs from. It was you that night, when I ran from Jeremy. I understood, then, why you'd written the letter. I could even sympathize with your need for revenge."

Revenge? Perhaps that had been his intention at the start, but somewhere along the way, his motives had altered.

"Especially considering your bet," she went on. "It had to be awful, contemplating your horses in Fortesque's hands. I understand, truly. And you needn't feel remorse for fostering any undue expectations. Any reasonable female would know better than to refine overmuch on such a note."

Now that stung. "What was wrong with my letter?"

"Nothing." As if surprised, she paused over the cup. "It was a perfectly sensible statement of intention but anyone could see it was not the words of a man in love."

Her hands moved in increasing speed as she filled those unwanted cups, as if the movement could disguise her inner tension. It didn't elude Geoff, for he felt the same nervousness himself.

He took her hands, forcing her to abandon the ladle. She merely blinked at him, then looked down at their joined fingers. She did not wear gloves, he now noticed, her hands were chilled and trembling visibly.

Forcing her chin up, he gazed into her startled eyes. How unfair he'd been to blame her for running away, when all his life, he'd run from everything he didn't wish to face. Even now, he had an overwhelming urge to flee rather than risk her rejection.

Yet when Honor tried to pull away, he found himself tightening his grasp. For the first time in his life, he'd found something worth fighting for. Whatever the battle, he was not going to let her slip away.

"I'm sorry my letter was not overly romantic," he told

her, "but in all your reasoning and understanding, did you never try reading between the lines?"

As her eyes searched his, he probed for the words to convince her. Drat, he should have read Byron, or listened when his friends talked of wooing their ladies.

Yet deep down, he knew that wasn't what Honor would wish at all. She'd want a prince to sweep her away. Some bold soul to go down on his knee and tell the world just how much he loved her.

Taking a deep breath, he took the plunge. He went to his knee, grasping her hands tighter, as if determined to keep her there until he'd had his say. "Deuce take it, Honor, can't you see that I adore you madly?"

She bit her lip. Blinking resolutely, she looked away. "How can you do this?"

"What's wrong?" He glanced over his shoulder. "Isn't this public enough?"

"Please, do not make sport of me."

She might stand there with a stiff spine and upraised chin, but all the same, she was about to cry. There and then, Geoff decided that he would rather suffer a thousand rejections than ever see her this way again. "Look at me, dammit. Can't you see I'm asking you to be my wife?"

She did look at him, her eyes disbelieving. "You can't be thinking logically. I know how you feel about appearances and . . ." she paused to glance around them, ". . . I'm too unconventional to ever be accepted by the ton."

"Hang the ton, and hang convention, too. I wouldn't be dirtying my knees if I cared a fig for what others think about your misadventures. To be perfectly candid, I'd as soon be a part of your escapades than feel as alone as I've been these past few weeks without you. You've got to marry me, Honor. I need you beside me for the rest of my life."

"Oh, Geoff, I . . ."

Before she could say more, a cane poked Geoff in the back. "Get up off your knees, boy. You're making a spectacle of yourself."

"What of it? I will not stand until I have my answer."

"Yes." Honor's smile seemed to light up the room. "Oh, Geoff, yes."

He rose then, and would have gathered her in his arms, but the cane came to rest between them. "My farthing, if you don't mind," Lady Sarah demanded.

Geoff happily placed the coin in her palm. He was quite willing to sacrifice the Pithnevel Pearls to his cousins as well. Gazing down at Honor, he knew he had won the greatest prize of all.

"I still have that special license," he told Honor, his eyes never leaving her face. "We shall have to consult with the general, of course, but for myself, I don't wish to waste a day."

"Nor do I." She too seemed to find it impossible to look away. "I keep worrying that this is all a dream from which I shall too soon have to wake."

"Then I shall just have to dash in and sweep you off. Nothing quite so enjoyable as rescuing a damsel in distress, I found."

Lady Sarah snorted. "I can't say I enjoy watching you, so save such nonsense for when you are alone." She gestured with her cane. "For the present, if you can't keep your hands off her, I suggest you lead Honor out onto the dance floor. You might as well start the process, for I daresay she'll be leading you a merry dance in the years to come."

Grinning, Geoff held out his arm, more than happy to see Honor kick up her heels again. Heaven help him, but would he ever tire of seeing her smile?

Leading Honor off, he did not bother to tell Lady Sarah that he had no intention of wasting the afternoon on the

dance floor. It was customary, he'd been told, to seal a betrothal with a kiss, and he knew of a small room down the
hall where they could be quite alone.

Sarah watched the dancing couples, reminding herself
that it was soon time to announce the twins' weddings.
Removing Foxley and Bellington from the Marriage Mart
would not please the Pithnevel girls, but they deserved to
be disappointed for trying to keep Honor and Lennox
apart.

Thinking of her goddaughter, Sarah looked for Honor,
but all she saw was the girl's back as Lennox hurried her
out of the room. He knew the house well, Sarah thought,
stifling a grin; he should be finding them privacy soon
enough.

Another wedding in the works. Sighing happily, she
knew she deserved to feel pleased with herself. It was
quite some accomplishment, joining first Richard and
Andrea, and now Lennox and Honor.

But just who, she wondered as she raised her quizzing
glass to inspect the dancing couples, would be next?